CUCKOO
Avner Mandelman

We acknowledge the support of the Canada Council for the Arts, the Ontario Arts Council, the Government of Ontario through the Ontario Media Development Corporation's Ontario Book Initiative and the Government of Canada through the Book Publishing Industry Development Program for our publishing activities.

"Cuckoo" and "Take-Down" were originally published in *Parchment*. "Cuckoo" has been shortlisted for the Journey Prize and will appear in *The Journey Prize Anthology*. "Dybbuk" was first published in the *University of Waterloo Quarterly*.

ISBN 0 7780 1238 7 (hardcover)
ISBN 0 7780 1239 5 (softcover)

ONTARIO ARTS COUNCIL
CONSEIL DES ARTS DE L'ONTARIO

Cover art by Barbara Carter
Book design by Michael Macklem

Printed in Canada

PUBLISHED IN CANADA BY OBERON PRESS

Contents

To my parents

Cuckoo

My cousin Yochanan who lost an eye in the Six Day War left Israel in 1968, soon after, and went to America to make money. He stayed on Wall Street 22 years, working, as they say, like a donkey, and so never had time to get married. Or maybe he didn't want to; because though he had lots of offers, including a beauty queen (New Jersey, 1987), and two El-Al stewardesses, he was afraid they were all after his money, which maybe was true, because in the meantime he had become a partner at Loewenstein Brothers, and was worth maybe four or five million dollars, plus his partnership interest. Finally in 1990 on a visit to Israel, to see his mother (that's my father's sister Rivka), he also dropped in on my father in his tailor shop on Nachalat Binyamin Street, to talk, and to make a new suit (it's cheaper than Brooks Brothers), and there he met Pnina Chelnov, the daughter of Sarah Chelnov, the "1956 Nightingale" who had sung the famous "Nights of Blood," and who now gave her skirts to my father to be taken out or in, depending on her diet.

Now, Sarah's daughter Pnina was only 24 years old, sixteen years younger than Yochanan, and she had already been married once (for a year), to a Yemenite from Kerem HaTeymanim named Yig'al Z'ruya, who had divorced her because she couldn't have children. Pnina herself was half Yemenite—her mother, Sarah, was born in San'a, but had married Gavriel Chelnov, the comic actor, and had one child—Pnina, who, like most children of mixed marriages, was a beauty, with fair skin and tight curly hair, and with the rollicking walk of a Yemenite, but the legs of an Ashkenazi—everyone looked at her as she walked down the street, or came into the grocery store to buy bread, or eggs. So from here to there, Yochanan, who liked pretty girls—though not to get married with—forgot about the suit and took Pnina to lunch at Kerem HaTeymanim, of all places, and there, Pnina's ex-husband, who was a small-time criminal (diamond burglaries), saw them eating hummus together from one plate and got jealous—though what did he have to get jealous about? He and Pnina were divorced four years already!—so he slapped her on the face right at the table, before everybody.

From what I learned later, two policemen were also in the restaurant (having Turkish coffee), one from the anti-terrorist squad, the other from police intelligence, but none of them did anything, because why get tangled up in something not your business, and with a Yemenite, too? But Yochanan, who in the army had been with the paratroopers (as an officer, though only at the Supply warehouse, in Sarafend), got up, and immediately punched the ex-husband two times, once in the stomach, the other in the face, and broke his (the Yemenite's) nose.

Now, although the restaurant (Tziyon's, on the corner of Malkiel Street and Even-Chen) was full of Yemenites, from complete astonishment nobody did anything to Yochanan—later it came out that Pnina had said to someone that he (Yochanan) was a friend of Sammy Aboutboul, a Moroccan from the HaTiqva neighbourhood, who the year before had emigrated to America to start a small mafia in Brooklyn; or maybe it's a tall-tale, who knows. But the result was that Yochanan and Pnina finished their hummus (with Pnina holding a cold Tempo bottle to her cheek), and right after, she went with him to his suite at Dan Hotel, and the following week Yochanan told my father (who, ever since Yochanan's own father had died in '56 in the Kadesh campaign, was like a father to him), that he, Yochanan, was getting married.

"To whom?" asked my father, who already guessed, but hoped it wasn't true.

"To her," Yochanan said, "Pnina Chelnov, that I met through you, here."

8

My father later said he felt a cold hand on his heart, because, to make a Shiduch, a match, is a Mitzvah. But this? What's the point for Jews to get married? Only, begging your pardon, to go to bed? For this you don't need a ring. For this, begging your pardon again, even Shiksas are good, of which there are plenty in America. Jews get married to procreate, that's what for, like it says in the book of Genesis. But with Pnina a barren woman, and after a Yemenite, too (who most of them can make children even when they are 80), why put a healthy head into a sick bed, as they say?

But Yochanan did not want to hear anything. "In my age," he said, "when I finally found love, I will marry her, no matter what anybody says."

"Yochanan," my father told him, "listen to me. With your money, you can marry a Rabbi's daughter, even, to be a good Jewish wife to you, and make you five children, ten, even. What do you need this one for?"

But, as they say, when a mule has made up his mind, nothing helps. So nothing helped here either, and after maybe two weeks, in which Yochanan also met Pnina's family (her mother Sarah, and two uncles in Hadera), he left for America, and after another week he sent her an El-Al ticket (first class), and the next month they got married in the biggest synagogue on the upper West Side, right under his co-op apartment.

So that's how it began. For the next two years they lived there, in New York, and also in Florida, where Yochanan had a little sailboat, and a condo, and also every year they came to Israel to visit, and to see the family: from Pnina's side, her mother, and from Yochanan's side, us. (His mother died right after the marriage.)

Pnina in the meantime had begun working in El-Al's New York office, where Yochanan's chauffeur's used to bring her every morning, after he drove Yochanan to work, until she told him to stop, because no-one at work talked to her. She just wanted to be like everyone else.

Now if you ask me, I think Pnina was a good girl, and everything that happened was not her fault, both then, and later. Sometimes, like they say, God plays jokes, and people suffer. And who does He like to play jokes on, most? Exactly. The Jews.

So, like I said before, the only problem of Pnina was, she couldn't have children. Everything else, a husband, money, work, vacations, she had. Only no children. Not that she and Yochanan didn't try. They travelled everywhere, to the Caribbean, Paris, Gstaad, who knows where else, for the atmosphere, the air and the water, maybe something would help them relax. But nothing helped. Also, every year when they came to Israel, on Passover (usually they came to us, to the Seder), they also went to doctors, first in Ichilov and Hadassah hospitals, then private, but the doctors could do nothing. There was nothing wrong with either Yochanan or Pnina, they said. Just no children.

So after a while Pnina began to keep Kosher kitchen in her New York apartment, just in case, and go to synagogue, and visit holy Rabbis to get a blessing, or an amulet—I heard once that she had made Yochanan give maybe $10,000 (some say $100,000) to the Boyberisher Rebbe's charity, for a special amulet (a piece of paper with letters from the Kabbalah, and a clove of garlic and a coin inside). But again nothing helped. So then they began to talk about adopting, but of this also nothing came, because who knows who were the baby's parents? Maybe they were unmarried Jews, so he's a bastard? This can never be erased, to the tenth generation.

So finally finally, on one of the visits to Israel, a famous doctor in Hadassah found what was wrong with Pnina: her eggs were no good. Broken, or something. So no matter what, she would not be able to have children, amulets or no.

The very next day, Pnina came to my father's tailor shop and asked my father to go tell Yochanan she was offering him a Gett, so he, Yochanan, could at least get married with someone who could give him children.

My father did not want to give this message, because, first, in the meantime, barren or not barren, he had begun to like Pnina—because what was her fault if God decided to play such a cruel trick on her? And second, because while making a match is a Mitzvah, making a divorce is a sin. So not only did he make such a bad mistake introducing Yochanan to this poor barren woman, he would now also be the messenger for the divorce? So he told Pnina, why don't you wait, maybe God will take pity on you? But she had made up her mind, and said, No, go tell him, so finally my father did.

But, like you guessed, Yochanan did not want to hear from a Gett. Some evil tongues said it would have cost him too much money, because to get divorced in New York, is not like to get divorced in Tel Aviv. You are lucky if the wife leaves you a little shirt on your back. But I don't believe this. You only had to look at them, to see this was not a question of money, but real love for children. So again they talked about adoption, and my father said maybe he could ask from his friends on Lillienblum Street, that bought and sold gold, and Marks, and Dollars, to find where you can get a baby also, maybe in Be'er Sheva, or Magdi'el, where Russian immigrants, who had settled there, were usually willing to do things for money that no-one else would; but Pnina said no. She did not want to take anyone else's baby, to build her happiness on the misery of others. A Gett was the only solution.

But then Pnina's mother, Sarah Chelnov, came out and said, "I have another idea. I will do it for you."

"Do what?" said Pnina.

"I will carry your baby," Sarah said.

At first Pnina thought it was a bad joke. Because, let's

face it, Sarah was then already 40 years old (she had born Pnina when she was sixteen); and also, who had ever heard of such things? It was filth.

But then it came out Sarah hadn't meant she would, begging your pardon, go to bed with Yochanan. Just do it with a doctor, with a syringe. "Like an injection," she said.

At this both my father and mother said they didn't think it was possible, but Sarah said, they did it with cattle all the time.

"We are not cattle," my father said. "We are Zussmans."

Pnina, too, didn't want to hear from this. But after a while, little by little, it came out maybe it wasn't such a bad solution, because Sarah (who had just then begun recording again) had some free time, and was also not going out with anyone, and still had not, begging your pardon again, dried up as a woman. So, the following week, they all went to the lawyer Ya'acov Gelber, and wrote a contract (which Yochanan insisted on). Then the very next day they went, together with my father and mother, to Hadassah hospital, where Dr. Nissan Rivkin the gynaecologist (the brother of the famous Pesach Rivkin, who wrote the articles about cancer), did what they asked.

Then Yochanan and Pnina went back to America, and waited.

This was the end of 1991, and the stock market was going crazy, so Yochanan busied himself with this, while Pnina did nothing but call her mother, to check, every day. But somehow the injection didn't catch, so after two months, Yochanan left the stock market and he and Pnina came back; and once again, they did it with Pnina's mother, and with Dr. Divkin; and this time they waited in Tel Aviv, in Dan Hotel, for the result; but once more it didn't catch. So again, they did it with Dr. Rivkin, and went to America to wait—it went like this for six more months, with no results, and they almost despaired, until Pnina said, "maybe you just have to do it the way it should be done."

At first Yochanan thought she was joking, but she wasn't. So, to cut a long story, it also came out she had already talked to her mother, and she (her mother) already agreed, but she (her mother) wasn't sure if Yochanan would. Not because she, Sarah, was ugly (she wasn't), but because in the meantime, he, Yochanan, had become religious in America, and an adherent of the Boyberisher Rebbe, to whose court he was going every Saturday to partake of the Rebbe's table, and to pray, because of Pnina.

So, to cut it even shorter, Yochanan decided to put all this question before the Boyberisher Rebbe himself.

Now, normally, to get to see the Boyberisher for even a minute, is a miracle. Because, as is well known, from even one word of his mouth, the Heavens open. But with Yochanan, who for two years already was coming to the Rebbe's table, and was also giving in secret to the Boyberisher orphanage, there happened a special exception, and he got to see the Rebbe for a whole half-hour. Almost like Rabin, or Peres, when they come to New York. So of course evil tongues began to wag, and said the Rebbe did it because he, Yochanan, gave money, and maybe he also would give more; but this is not true, because some Jews (like the Bronskys, or the Loewensteins) much richer never got to see the Rebbe even for five minutes.

Anyway, no-one knows what the Rebbe and Yochanan talked about, but the result was that Yochanan gave Pnina a Gett, written specially by the Boyberisher himself, then flew to Israel, where he went to see her mother. What they did nobody knows, because maybe they again went to Dr. Rivkin? Who can say for sure that they didn't? But the outcome was, that Sarah became pregnant, and nine months later she gave birth to two boys; and Yochanan and Pnina, who got married again, adopted them. Then Yochanan and Pnina and the two boys all came to live in Tel Aviv (on

13

Maz'eh Street), where Lowenstein Brothers had just opened a branch for investment in Israeli Hi Tech, and Yochanan was the partner in charge.

Now if you think that this is the end of the story, you are mistaken. Because the following year, right after Sarah Chelnov's new record came out (with 1956 songs, accompanied by a flute and a rababeh), Pnina's mother went cuckoo. At first no-one realized this (because she only stopped cleaning her apartment, and washing the dishes), until she began to scream in the night that her happiness had arrived, but she gave it up. The neighbours asked her to stop shouting; then, when this didn't help, they called Pnina and Yochanan.

At first Yochanan and Pnina thought, this was because she had given up the babies. So they came often, with the boys, so Sarah could play with them, more like a mother than a grandmother (even though, as you can imagine, Pnina didn't like this), but soon it became obvious that who Sarah was after was not the boys, but Yochanan.

This was 1992, and Yochanan was 42 years old, only one year older than Sarah, and looked good because he also did exercises (like running every morning on the Gordon beach, or lifting weights), and even if he had only one eye, he didn't put glass in it, only covered it up with a black patch, like Moshe Dayan, who, as everyone knew, was once Sarah's boyfriend. So, what can I say, Yochanan and Pnina just took the kids back to Maz'eh Street, and stopped coming; but then Sarah, who was not cuckoo enough to be put in the Bat Yam asylum (where there's never enough room), started coming to ring their doorbell in Maz'eh, or write letters to Yochanan and slip it under the door, or even cook hummus (for Yochanan), and leave it on the doormat, in a pot, again with notes.

Finally Pnina couldn't take this anymore, and she made

Yochanan take her back to New York, with the children. And right after, her mother one night began to scream and sing so loud, that finally the neighbours called an ambulance, and because Bat Yam was full, she was taken to Beit Tzedek hospital, in Jerusalem, where someone who had once heard her sing in '56 was now a doctor; then for a while no-one knew anything else.

This was already 1993, and the stock market was not so crazy anymore, so Yochanan had some time on his hands. So again he began to go to the Boyberisher court, and from here to there, he became one of the helpers of Rabbi Shlomo Tzirelsohn, the Boyberisher minister of finance, so to speak. This job he, Yochanan, of course did for free, for the Mitzvah; but free or not, little by little he began to give more time to the Rebbe, and less to Loewenstein Brothers. He also began to grow his sidelocks, and wear the black clothes of the Boyberisher Chassidim; and Pnina, even though she was keeping a kosher kitchen, and everything, did not like this very much. Because, let's face it, now that she had the boys, what did she need to be so religious for? Also, don't forget, she was only 29, maybe, so did she want to bury herself in the kitchen doing kosher? No. She wanted to go see shows on Broadway, maybe a concert, and movies. But now Yochanan did not have the time, or the will, to go. So from here to there, no-one knows how it happened, Pnina one day met someone, in Brooklyn, and who do you think it was? No, not her ex-husband the Yemenite, but Sammy Aboutboul, who did not open a mafia after all, and was only moving furniture, with a truck. So from here to there, they started talking, about Tel Aviv, and soccer games (which Pnina used to go to, before she met Yochanan), then they sat down to have Falafel (on Seventh Avenue and 83rd), and finally Sammy asked if he could call her again, and she said, Okay, but only to talk.

And that's how it started. After a while, when Yochanan

was spending even more time at the Boyberisher court (he no longer worked for Lowenstein Brothers—but he had enough money so he didn't have to), and Pnina said she was going out shopping (by that time they already had a nanny, from the Philippines)—she really went out to see Sammy.

After maybe six months of this, it all came out, because someone who had seen Pnina with Sammy, in a movie, sent a letter—not to Yochanan, but to Rabbi Shlomo Tzirelsohn, for whom Yochanan was now working, for free, at the Boyberisher court; and in the letter, the evil tongues pretended they only had Yochanan's welfare at heart (else how could they allow themselves to write such a thing?) and asked Rabbi Tzirelsohn to give Yochanan some time off, so he could take care of his young wife, to prevent her from committing sin.

Because the Boyberisher was sick then, Rabbi Tzirelsohn couldn't ask his advice, so on his own idea he showed the letter to Yochanan. And when Yochanan read this, he took off his Kapota, and his hat, and took a cab straight home. There he slapped Pnina like she had never been slapped before, and then he went back to Brooklyn to see Sammy Aboutboul. And there, even though Sammy was maybe 36, and Yochanan, eight years older, and Sammy was lifting pianos and sofas and tables every day, and Yochanan, just doing calculations, he, Yochanan, beat Sammy up so bad, that the neighbours had to call the police, and the police took him, Yochanan, to jail.

Now, listen to this: when Yochanan got out (due to special intercession on the part of the Rebbe, who in the meantime had gotten well), he saw that Pnina was not home—(later it came out she had gone to see Sammy, at the hospital)—and the children she left with the nanny. So without saying anything, Yochanan took the children, packed two suitcases, and called a cab to the airport. But there, instead of

16

buying regular air tickets, he went to the private jet lounge, and asked the Lowenstein Brothers' pilot (the firm had two jets, both Astras, made in Israel) to take him and the children special to Israel. (As ex partner, he could use the plane, but he had to pay for it.)

When Pnina came back, and saw that the children were gone, she immediately called the police, and they alerted the airport, to look for a man with two children, going to Israel. But, like I said, Yochanan took the private jet of his old firm, so the very next day he landed in Lod, where no-one knew of anything, so they let him in.

And where do you think he went? You are right, straight to the apartment of Sarah Chelnov, Pnina's mother.

Now, I already said that, right after Pnina and Yochanan had left, because Sarah Chelnov had gone crazy, she was taken to Beit Tzedek hospital in Jerusalem. But after maybe two weeks there, she got well enough to be let out. But instead of returning to Tel Aviv immediately, she went first to Me'a Sh'arim, which is the most orthodox neighbourhood in Jerusalem, and went in to see Rabbi Ury Blisker, who in those days was the first Rabbi everyone who wanted to become religious went to. To no-one's surprise, Rabbi Blisker told her to start keeping kosher kitchen, and to go to synagogue, and to give to charity, but also to go back to Tel Aviv, not to stay in Jerusalem. When she asked if she should also continue to sing, and make records, he said yes, but also to make records of songs from the bible.

So what can I tell you? You probably know the rest. Sarah Chelnov then made a record (in November 1994) of the Song of Songs, together with a choir of simple Yemenites from the street, all kinds of verses, with melodies by Ne'omi Sharf, Nechemia Malchin, the Chamdi brothers, and others; and she sold maybe 50,000 copies of this, which in Israel is unheard-of. And from this money, she gave half to Yeshivot, and to orphanages, in Beny Barak and in Jerusalem, so people bought even more records; and even religious people, who never listen to music, they bought also. So to make a long story really short, Sarah Chelnov became again a success, like she was once in 1956, and also became happy again, with synagogue, and prayer, and singing.

The only thing she didn't want to do, was get married with any one of the widowers or the divorced Rabbis that Ury Blisker kept sending her (because it is a sin for a person to be alone, if he can make a Jewish family, and it's a Mitzvah to make a Shiduch, a match). But other than that, and the fact she no longer talked to her daughter, or her children, it was not the worst.

So it was then (this was January, 1995), that Yochanan came to her apartment, with the two children, straight from the airport.

What happened right after, I don't know exactly. My father said that, at first, Sarah Chelnov said, Don't stay here, it'll be a sin: You are married to someone else. But Yochanan said, I'll sleep in the other room, but I stay here, because the children should be with their family, not strangers. So finally she agreed. But my mother, who says she heard this from Sarah's own grocer, insists that at the beginning Yochanan and the children did not even come to Sarah's apartment, but went instead to hotel Z'vulun, which is the place all the Orthodox Jews go to, two blocks from Dan Hotel; and only after two weeks, when Yochanan finally got the Gett (he received it from the Beit Din, the Rabbinical Court, of the Chabadniks in Bney Barak, saying he had a rebel wife), did he finally go to live with Sarah, together with the children.

But if you listen to the evil tongues (especially in Ha'Olam HaZeh magazine, where the gossip column is full of stories), this wasn't at all how it happened, because (that's what some of the stories say), it was Pnina who had left

Yochanan, and only after she had discovered he was secretly corresponding with her mother, and promising to come see her, Sarah, soon. If you ask me? I don't know what's true. What I know is, after three days Pnina arrived from New York to Tel Aviv, and immediately hired the best lawyer, David Kupershnit (who was once assistant to the Minister of Justice), and sued Yochanan for custody of the children.

Now this really started the evil tongues going. Because, can you imagine? First there was the chance that Yochanan's talk with the Boyberisher would come up in court, and he would have to tell everything about the advice he got. Then, of course, out would come the answer if he and Sarah did do it like a husband and wife, or not; which nobody knew. And also would come out the part about Pnina and Sammy—who, after a little while, it came out did start a little Mafia, and the moving business was only a cover. And if this was not enough, Pnina just then became pregnant, from Sammy, so she claimed she could provide the boys as good a home as Yochanan and her mother could.

What can I tell you? All this was so good and juicy, that for a whole month, even though Rabin was just then negotiating with the Religious parties to go into the coalition, no-one in Tel Aviv (also in other big cities) was talking of anything else. There was even a little fight among the judges, about who would sit in the case. Finally Judge Sorokin, who was about to retire, got it, and he began hearing evidence on March 1995, in the new courtroom in Ramat Gan (the old family court, on Aliya Street, had just closed, in 1993).

Then everything stopped. Because, in the blood test, which they had to do, for the boys, it came out they were not Yochanan's at all. Can you imagine? At first, the lawyers did not know what to do, until Judge Sorokin (who did not get to be Chief Judge of the Appelate Court of the Dan District for nothing) said he wanted a blood test of everyone in the courtroom, who came to watch. For this he was ridiculed for maybe a week, in all the newspapers; until it came out that the blood-type that was the same as the boys was that of Pnina's ex-husband, the Yemenite, Yig'al Z'ruya. But because blood-type by itself doesn't mean much, the judge also ordered this new DNA test, for the ex-husband, and the entire trial stopped, for ten days, until came back the answer from the FBI lab in Cincinnati, that no question, Pnina's ex-husband, Yig'al Z'ruya, was the boys' father.

Now this became worse and worse. Because, just think of it, when did Sarah have time to meet him? Or did she maybe go to ask him in secret to fill the syringe, instead of Yochanan? Why? Besides, why would he? Then, finally, when they began to question Sarah, it came out that she did met this Yig'al Z'ruyah in the Carmel market, after maybe the third or forth injection, from Yochanan, and later also once in the Yemenite choir for her record, so maybe something happened, but she did not remember.

Now, when came out this, that the boys were really Pnina's ex-husband's, it really got complicated, because Yiga'l Z'ruya then got himself also a lawyer (Amnon Braverman, who last month was indicted for bribing a government minister), and said he, too, wanted custody. And because he, also, in the meantime had remarried, and had two children already (twins), and since he hasn't been in jail for already two and half years, he, too, he said, could provide a good home for the boys.

Now, during all this, Yochanan and Sarah went on living together, but it was no longer peaceful. Whether it was because of what came out about Pnina's ex-husband, and Sarah Chelnov, or whether because Pnina and her mother were now fighting both over Yochanan, and over the boys, who knows. Probably everything together.

But what really threw everything into a loop, was that,

with all the blood tests being done, and the DNA tests, and everything, Pnina, who was now pregnant in the seventh month, decided to do a blood test also. And who do you think she found out was the father of her child? You are right. Yochanan. It came out that two months before she left him, in New York, they had once tried to make up (because the Boyberisher told them), and this was the result. So is God playing sick jokes on people, or what? I don't want to answer this, but if you want to, go ahead.

And how did this all finish?

At the end, Judge Sorokin did something that made just about everybody mad at him: he stopped the trial, and took everyone into chambers, and put fifteen policemen around the court, at every window, so no-one could peek in, or listen, and for seven hours he and all the litigants tried to come to some kind of arrangement.

But what it was, nobody knows. The only thing known is that, maybe three, four times a year, Sarah Chelnov (who in the meantime had married Sammy Aboutboul, who is now her manager) and her new baby, flies to Florida from Tel Aviv, and also Yig'al Z'ruya and his new wife, and their children, and they all spend maybe a week with Yochanan and Pnina, and the three boys; and some of the children sometimes stay there, or sometimes they stay in Tel Aviv, with us. My father also was invited once to go to Florida, but he said he can't go, because, first, at his age (73) he doesn't know if he should fly in airplanes for the first time, he could come back in a coffin. And, second, if by mistake he makes another cuckoo shiduch like this one it'll be even worse, why help God mock us again? When God plays a joke on us Jews, he says, the only thing to do is take care of the children hurt by Him and refuse to laugh; because unfortunately it is not permissible to play a joke on Him right back.

Black

My father's cousin Baruch who worked as a butcher in Tel Aviv's Carmel market, married a Moroccan cleaning-woman seven years older, and was immediately cut off from the family. Not because she was older—my own mother is four years older than my father—nor because she was a cleaning-woman—my father, after all, was a balegooleh, a mule driver—but because she was a schwartze, black; a Moroccan Jewess. Her name was Pirchiyah Azoulai, and as a matter of fact she was born in Israel, but the rest of her family had come from Fez, in the Atlas mountains in Morocco. So that's what they were. In Israel they lived in a small village near Be'er Sheva, where Pirchiyah's father, Leon Azoulai, was a lay Rabbi, and her mother, Freha, a spell-woman who, so it was said, still did Moroccan black-magic on the side. But one of Pirchiyah's sisters had married an army paratroop major, and a brother of hers worked in the Interior Ministry as assistant Kashrut inspector. Still, she was a Moroccan, a schwartze, and we, Ashkenazi, white. What's more, my own grandfather, Yechezke'el Leib Zalmanovitch (after whom I am named), a balegooleh like my father, had been an early disciple of the first Boyberishe Rebbe, whom he used to drive to Polish villages to waken up slumbering Jewish souls; and my mother, though a daughter of a fish-grocer from Krakow, was from her side also not without distinction: her grandfather, Moshe-Chaim Bloom, a bookbinder, had once visited the Holy Ari of Safed, the great Kabbalist, and later wrote a match-making guide with simple spells from the Kabbalah (which my mother claims she had learned at his knee).

A Moroccan in our family was clearly out of the question.

"We have Yechezke'el to think of," my father said.

In secret, though, my mother still went to see Baruch, in his butcher-shop in the Carmel market, and occasionally even bought from him a beef shank, or a plucked chicken. But neither he nor his wife were invited to weddings, circumcisions or Bar Mitzvahs.

"Or we'd have to invite them all," said my father.

At first Baruch said he didn't care. "You don't want me, fine. I'll go to hers." Meaning Pirchiyah's family. But after a few years, most likely prodded by his wife, who in the meantime had borne him four children, he came one day to our apartment on Bazel Street and said to my father, "Listen. Me, all right. Keep out if you want. But my children, invite them at least? What have they sinned, that they can't sit with their family? They are his cousins!" Meaning mine.

"You should have thought of it before," said my father.

Now all this took place in 1970, just before my own Bar Mitzvah, which was supposed to be a big thing—I had just had a bout with scarlatina, when my father made a vow before the Holy Ark to spend 1,000 Lirot on the festivity, if I recovered. When I did, my mother rented the largest hall under the Maxim cinema, and engaged rabbi Simcha Tuvim of the Bugrashov synagogue to teach me the reading of the Torah. (It was the Scroll of Eicha, I recall, where the Maiden of Zion is consoled by the prophet Yechezke'el, who tells her that one day it will all be set aright.) All my father's cousins from Canada and New York were invited, and my mother's family from Bney Barak, although the balegooleh friends of my father were not. (My father had stopped driving a cart the year before, and now had three carts, which he rented out to others.) Every day I practiced my Reading, and also a Kreizler sonata on my violin, for the guests. Once a week I went to Nachum Litvak the tailor, to have my measurements re-taken, for my first long pants and jacket; and gifts began arriving: a Motorola transistor radio from America, and, from Canada, an Omega wristwatch with seventeen stones and a wallet with thirteen Canadian dollars in it, in bills of fives and ones. Then my father, one week before the Torah Reading, took me to Kalman's bicycle store on the corner of Bar Cochba and Dizzengoff, and let me pick a three-speed red Raleigh, with a tilting seat, and after he had paid, marched me to Bergman's kiosk across the street, had Yossef Bergman place two chairs on the sidewalk, and ordered two coffees—one for him, one for me. It was my first.

"You are going to be a mensch soon," my father said, slurping his coffee, which he drank with lots of milk.

"Sure," I said, slurping mine proudly.

Everything seemed set. Even my violin no longer squeaked in the last part of the sonata. Then one week before my Bar Mitzvah, Pirchiyah came to see my father.

It was a Friday eve when she arrived, and we had already finished the Shabbat meal. My mother had washed the dishes, and my father, wearing an apron, was drying them at the sink when Pirchiyah knocked on the door, and without waiting for an answer, entered. Her long hair was loose, she wore purple trousers and gave off a strong smell of soap.

"I want to talk to you," she said to my father.

My mother looked at her, then at my father, and wrung her hands.

My father said, "Not in front of the child."

"Yes in front," said Pirchiyah. "Why not? Let him know."

"I beg of you," said my mother.

"Out," said my father, extending his hand in a gesture of divine expulsion. "Out of my house!"

"Shmiel," said my mother. "Let her speak at least."

"Speak what?"

"I have a message," said Pirchiyah. "From my mother."

"A message? So rejoice!" said my father. "A message from the machasheyfa."

The last word he said in Yiddish; it means both a witch and a shrew.

"I beg of you," my mother said again, not making clear whether she had meant Pirchiyah, my father, or both.

Pirchiyah said, "And if you don't, you'll see."

There was a short pause. My mother said, "All the invitations are already—"

"Not for me," said Pirchiyah, "for them."

And one by one, from behind her, the four children filed in: handsome and odd-looking, the two boys with Pirchiyah's tight curly hair but Baruch's fair skin, the two girls with dark skin and blond tresses.

They stood by the wall, in a line, as if they had practised it.

"So what will she do?" said my father. "Bring up Ashmedai?" He laughed out loud.

"Please, Shmiel!" cried my mother.

My father said, "I'm a balegooleh, not a Moroccan."

There was a tense pause. Pirchiyah's face contorted. At first I thought she would shout, or argue, or cry, but she did none of these things. Instead, from a pocket in her pants she pulled out a little jar, and unscrewed the top.

"What—" my father began, then he jumped to push me away, but it was too late. Pirchiyah had sprinkled the jar's contents on me—it was either blood (chicken's, probably), or some other thick liquid—and recited quickly something in a high-pitched voice.

My mother screamed.

"If my children can't be there," hissed Pirchiyah, "then neither will he," and one by one she and her children filed out, the eldest daughter bringing up the rear.

My father rushed to the hall, and shouted after them, that she should stay in the Carmel market, with the rest of the Schwartzes, not come to his home to do dirty Moroccan black magic. "Not even for a Shiv'a!" he hollered. "You hear? Not even for a Shiv'a!"

25

The stink of the red liquid was so overpowering—it seemed to have stuck to my hair, to my clothes, to my hands—that it took nearly an hour to wash it off. My mother stripped me naked and gave me a long bath, scrubbing me with a fresh lufa, crying all the while. I retched twice into the bath-water, and my mother brought me tea, with a spoonful of Carmel benediction wine, which she made me drink even as I sat in the water. Then she tucked me in bed, covering me with her own down blanket.

"Tomorrow you'll forget about it," she said, still crying. "You'll see."

But the next day I came down with fever. Dr. Gottlieb came to the house, and said there was a chance the scarlatina would return.

"Just keep him in bed," he said, "and plenty of tea."

"It's not scarlatina!" my mother wailed, when he had left. "It's from her!—Shmiel—go to her, beg her pardon—"

"Never in the world," said my father, adding inexplicably, "you want maybe to give the land back to the Arabs also?"

My mother grabbed his shirt. "You want your son to read the Torah next week? Yes or no."

"He'll read," said my father. "He'll read. With 40 degrees fever he'll read!"

But that afternoon my fever soared above 41 degrees, and I was rushed to Hadassah hospital. My father drove me there himself, in a cart hitched to his best mule.

"You stay with him," said my mother, "in case she comes back."

Both ended staying, sitting by my bedside.

That night I became delirious. Black soldiers with enormous shoes emerged from under my bed, marching straight into the wall where they were swallowed by a red mouth ringed by black eyes. The ceiling, its rim fading into dark nothingness, rotated viciously, first one way, then another. I woke up to see two nurses pressing socks with crushed ice to my forehead and neck. A doctor pushed a swab down my throat, then made me swallow a large sulfa capsule.

The next two days I received more sulfa, and injections. Rabbi Simcha Tuvim came to my bedside, wrapped in a prayer shawl, and said Tehillim over me, staring into the wall.

In spite of the sulfa, my fever lingered. The Bar Mitzvah had to be postponed.

"Go to her, Shmiel!" my mother wailed. "Ask her to come!"

"Never!"

"Don't be a mule!"

"No!"

My mother grabbed his hand. "If we cancel," she cried, "it'll cost 700 lirot. At least!"

My father put a fresh ice-filled sock on my forehead.

My mother went on, "The family will go back to Canada, and America—"

"No! I said no!"

"Then next month we'll have to do it only with the bale-goolehs—"

There was a long silence.

My father stood up.

"All right," he rasped, his cheeks dark. "But I'm doing it for you!"

My mother sobbed. "And for him?"

"For you only," said my father, not looking at me. "When he grows up and goes to the army he'll understand."

I couldn't see what the army had to do with it; but many things I did not understand then.

That evening Pirchiyah came to the hospital, Baruch silent at her side. He remained standing, while she sat at my bedside, and touched my forehead with a hand smelling of laundry soap.

"How are you, Yechezke'el?" Her voice was guttural, the glottals as deep as those of a radio announcer.

I swallowed through my constricted throat.

"Fine..." I croaked.

"Here, swallow this—" and before my mother could stop her, Pirchiyah had placed a folded piece of paper on my tongue, propped my head with one hand, and brought a glass of water to my lips with the other.

Confused, I swallowed.

My mother grabbed my chin, forcing my mouth open. But the paper had gone down already.

"What is it?" she shouted.

"An amulet," said Pirchiyah, "from her."

My mother said, "Aren't you ashamed of what you've done to him?"

Pirchiyah said, "What you want for him, I want for mine."

"This we shall see," said my mother.

There was a pause.

My father said, "I already invited them—"

"So you invited," said my mother.

That night my fever broke. My Bar Mitzvah had been postponed, but only by one week—most of my father's Canadian and American cousins remained, only three had left, and my father invited three balegoolehs in their place. He also invited Baruch and Pirchiyah, and their children, and Pirchiyah's parents.

It was the first time that I had seen them: Pirchiyah's mother was an enormously fat woman in a flowery dress, with black eyes rimmed with red, and a faint plume of a moustache, who sat in her corner the entire evening and knitted skullcaps. Pirchiyah's father was as small as a Yemenite, with a scraggly beard and a thin hook nose. Not once did I see him raise his eyes—he just ate and ate.

Pirchiyah and Baruch ate nothing—they just danced to the Kleizmer music, non-stop. But their children did eat, all except the eldest (whose name, I later learned, was Sarina) who sat between her grandparents, placid and observant like her grandmother, staring at me keenly all the while (my cheeks slowly heating under her gaze), as I thanked my father and mother in a speech, as I played the violin, as I later sat and ate double and triple helpings.

But just as I was about to launch into the compote, she suddenly rose to her feet, came up to our table, and asked if she could sit beside me.

My mother smiled at her thinly. "Why?" she asked.

"Because when I grow up I'll marry him."

My mother's smile disappeared.

I looked up in confusion, my heart seizing with wild heat. "Me?" I asked. "Why?"

"Because you are for me." She quickly sat down beside me, took out a folded paper packet, and sprinkled some powder on my compote bowl, which I was then raising to my lips. "Drink it."

"No!" cried my mother. "No!"

But it was too late—I had drunk up, quickly, and Sarina had left to join her grandmother, who now raised her eyes and gave me a large warm smile.

My mother then did something I'll never forget.

In front of everyone, the kleizmer orchestra, the waiters, my father's American and Canadian cousins, her own family from Bney Barak, she grabbed my head, clamped it under her armpit, forced my mouth open with her thumbs, and stuck two fingers down my throat.

"Out with it!" she hissed into my face. "All of it!"

I struggled—the fingers digging into my throat were like hot snakes—but my head seemed stuck in concrete. Helplessly I vomited, throwing up the chicken gizzards, the gefilte fish, the soup, the calf tongue in tomato sauce, the prune compote. I threw up on the table, upon my mother's new pink dress, on my father's blue suit—he just sat there, unmoving—and on my own.

When I finished retching, my mother gave me a glass of water.

"Now drink," she said, not even looking at me.

All dancing, all music, all talking, every movement or sound in the hall, had stopped. There was an odd, tingling silence, broken by my sobs.

Then, across the room, Pirchiyah's mother folded her knitting and slowly stood up; and right after her, Pirchiyah's father, then Baruch and Pirchiyah herself, and the children.

Pirchiyah's grandmother opened her mouth to speak, but no voice came out.

My mother was staring at her with eyes as black and red-rimmed as hers.

"Not in my home," she said. "Out!"

And that was it. A year later Baruch and Pirchiyah left Tel Aviv, with the children, and went to live in Dimonah, where Baruch went to work for HaMashbir, as a food clerk, while Pirchiyah found work as a cook in the Nuclear reactor, or perhaps in the Hawk missile battery guarding it. I no longer remember. No-one in the family talked to either of them much, though I once saw Pirchiyah with her daughter in Tel Aviv, coming out of a cheap clothing store —I think the daughter was Sarina. She had grown very tall —taller than me, and, like her grandmother, had large black eyes and a faint moustache; but this, like her long blond hair, seemed oddly out of place on her dark-olive skin. She looked at me without recognition while I nodded at her mother.

I was about to go into cinema Yaron, with Nurit, my then girlfriend, when I saw them. I was in my Air Force uniform, a pilot cadet, and very proud of it.

"Who's she?" asked Nurit, not making clear whether she had meant Pirchiyah, or her daughter.

"Used to be our cleaning lady," I said. "In Bazel Street."

To my surprise I felt neither guilt nor shame at the lie. And this was strange, because I had always thought of myself as free from prejudice.

Take-Down

It began as a routine take-down, nothing special. I was to go into Amman through Eastern Jerusalem to take down a Major in the Jordanian *muchabart* who had been catching too many of our 504 Unit patrolmen. In those days (this was 1966, one year before the Jordanian Legionnaires on the Abdallah bridge turned into border guards), our 504 Intel Unit guys used to go in with hand-held Hasselblad cameras once a week to photograph the goings-on in Q'arameh, A'salt, Shunat Nimrin, and all the other refugee camps infested with Palestinian *fedayeen*, to give us a heads up about the fuckers' plans. But this *muchabarat* Major was catching our photo patrols one after the other, like flies. So I received the order to go Across, take him down with a pencil-knife, then scoot South along the Arava road and come back In near kibbutz Yotvetta, where a *Charuv* Recon patrol would be waiting for me to take me to Be'er Sheva for a shower and a debrief.

Simple. Nothing much to it. Go Across, stick him, come back. At first I even thought this was just another test of the pencil-knife—the year before, a genius doctor in Hadassah Hospital had thought of it in his spare time, to help his country. It's a yellow neoprene tube with a thin tungsten wire inside, extremely thin but very stiff and held back with a spring. When you put it against a sleeping man's chest, then twist the top, the wire springs right in, and he never wakes up. The thing is, this wire-blade is so thin, it never leaves a mark, so in the morning it looks just like a heart attack. Now, at that time, the wire-knife was not yet thoroughly tested, so at first I thought this take-down in Amman was going to be just another test, because as far as I knew, our *shoo-shoo* likes to test everything three times before it accepts anything as standard O.P. But then, just before leaving for Jerusalem, I learned by complete chance from some secretary in *N'tivott*, the encryption department, that this job was not a test, but for real. That we really wanted this Major out. It seemed he had a source somewhere inside Israel, a shtinker who told him when a 504 Recon was going out, so it was not brilliance on his side, just gross negligence and stupidity on ours, and so something had to be done.

Selective false orders—to see where the leak was—were out of the question because this might have alerted the guy. So finally someone in the *Q'irya* in Tel Aviv had the brilliant idea it was better to do the opposite. First take this Major down directly, then wait and see who of the local Peaceniks, foreign diplomats, Israeli Arabs, and all others we routinely tailed here, scrambled to find out who his new controller was; who made too many phone calls; who acted nervous; whatever. It usually worked, and this time it did too; but that's not what I want to tell about. What I want to tell is what happened to me in Amman on this job. Because, let's face it, in those days I was still a little green, only two years after my military service (I had been in Unit 101 under Arik, before I transferred with him to the Paratroopers), a mere one year after take-down course, which I finished second (but first in knife-work), so I still did everything exactly like they told me to. Today, of course, if I got such orders I would've most probably first parked my ass on a few secretaries' desks, maybe taken one out for a fuck-and-tell, to learn the real story. That's how the place works. They expect you to show initiative both outside the Office and in. To be an unterweltmensh for your people. But, like I said, those days I was still a goody-goody soldier, a little Yoram, as they say in Tel Aviv, an obedient little mother's cunt. So after I had gotten my order's yellow-slip from Amnon Geller at the *N'tivott* department, I ran up to the briefing-room on the second floor where I pocketed all the maps they were willing to part with. Then a whole week I sat in Ramat Gan in the offices of *Akkavish* (that's how they

33

called then the department that controls *Katsas*, today it's *S'mamitt*), and, feeling as important as the Chief Sephardic Rabbi, went over the details, one by one, looking at the 504's photographs of the *muchabart* Major's house, his front yard, the hanging laundry at the back, the cactus hedges on both sides, roads of approach, everything. Finally when I knew it all by heart, where his kitchen was, where the bedroom, I gave all the maps back and returned to the Kfar Sirkin camp, to see if there was anything else. But there was nothing, and Geller said I could leave whenever I wanted.

"Just go do it," he said, "and bring back his prepuce."

This was a joke, of course. It refers to Kind David, who one night sneaked out and took down 50 Philistines, then cut off the tips of their dicks, as proof, and gave it all to King Shaul, who of course did not even say thanks.

"Nah, I'll bring in the dick whole," I said.

Geller gave me a punch in the shoulder, as customary, and said he would keep the newspaper's weekend supplement for me, with the sport section.

I punched him right back, and left him.

Still, just before I left the camp, I don't know why, I went to talk to Itzik Besser, a friend of mine from my 101 days. He was then at *Roshanim*, the department that dealt with the *Fedayeen*, (that's what they were called then, not PLO yet), tailing them, tracking those worth taking down. Because at that time the department was still very small, they occupied only one room at the end of the East building. Today they are of course spread over the three top floors, and, since the fuck-up in Munich with the eleven athletes, the entire *Kardomm* take-down unit (which has two entire floors directly below ground) practically reports to them. But in those days they were just beginning, so one room was enough.

Anyway, I went to see Itzik, without telling him anything of course, and together we went out to the West-wing cafeteria, to have a coffee. (One thing you can say about the *shoo-shoo*, no matter what unit you are in, the *hummus* is real *hummus*, and the coffee is good coffee, with real *hel*—cardamom seeds. It is said someone from the *Eytannim* department buys it in Cairo fresh every week.) So we sat in the canteen, Itzik and I, drinking Turkish coffee with *hel* in small porcelain cups and smoking Dubek cigarettes, and although he could probably see I was going Across, he didn't ask me anything, not a word. We just talked about the soccer win of Maccabi Natanya against HaPo'el Haifa, the recent hike in apartment taxes, the heatwave. I knew it was time for me to go, that I would be late arriving in Jerusalem if I didn't start out soon, but somehow I lingered.

I had gone to talk to Itzik because to my father I could not talk—he was second in line to Me'ir Ya'ari in *Mapam*, the leftist United Laborers' Party, so his office, like that of Ya'ari himself, was of course bugged. Besides, what could I say to him? We never seemed to have anything much to talk about anymore, ever since my mother had died two years before. Also at that time I was still not married, so I did not have a wife to talk to, and somehow all my friends were in such places that I could not talk to them either. Like Uzi Shimmel, from my class in Alliance High School, he was working in *Ha'aretz*, the leftist morning paper, and Tzuri Rivlin was in *Kol Yisrael*, the national radio station. Or Mickey Benevenisti, from Har N'vo school, he was now an actor in the *Cameri* theatre, and they had produced a few shows the military Censor did not like. Things like that.

Still, I don't know, like before every other take-down I felt I had to say goodbye to someone, anyone, because first of all, I was doing this for them. Also, let's face it, I was going into Amman, Jordan, and who knew what could happen there. Two guys from my take-down course (Uddy Fishbein and Gadi Yavneh) had already not come back, Uddy finished in Tadmor jail in Syria (suicide), and Gadi just never returned from a take-down in Iraq, nobody knows how or why. Some say the Tikriti bedouins caught him and buried him alive. But who knows.

So I just sat with Itzik and had a coffee with *hel*, and yakked on this and that, I don't know what about. Finally I got up, but when I was on my feet already, Itzik said, just like that, "If you get stuck, you know, give me a call, what do I know."

"I won't get stuck," I said.

Even this was too much to say, I knew. (I told you I was a Yoram then.) But he had lent me his ear for half an hour.

"So anyway," Itzik said, "if."

"All right," I said. "If."

Later I saw he had put a few cardamom seeds in my pocket—as if there is no *hel* in all of Amman. But what else could he give me. When two years later he went down in Qarameh, in '68, in that first big fight against the PLO (a big fuckup, if there ever was one), I cried, actually cried. And we were not even good friends, or anything.

But anyway, I left Itzik at the *N'tivott* cafeteria and took the bus to Jerusalem. When I arrived I did the usual *Maslool*, the operational evasive route, just in case *Akavish* had put a couple of Tailers on me, to see if I stayed sharp. But there was no-one. So I ate a leisurely siniyeh, sheep-ribs baked in taheena sauce, at a restaurant where they did not know me, then went straight to the Shin Bet H.Q. near the Muskobiya, the Russian Church, where at the time they were doing the Final Briefs before the Crossing. Even then it still did not seem like anything special, I must admit. I mean, no-one was waiting for me, I had to tell the bored Duty Officer who I was and he leafed for a whole minute through two notebooks before he found the name of my Briefer, a mere Captain in *Aman*, the Intelligence Corps, a staff guy who had compiled the last reports that had come in the night before from Across. He too seemed bored and tired. Probably in for a night duty instead of sleeping at home with his wife. A damn jobnik.

"He's been home all week," the captain said, "your Major. No suspicious activity."

"Like what, suspicious?" I said, just to make myself difficult.

We are supposed to be difficult to Aman people. It lets them know we are professional and demanding.

"Nothing, nothing suspicious," the captain said, still listless.

"All right," I said, and then, I don't know why, I said, "You want me to bring you anything, from there? Something?"

I don't know why I said that. I hardly knew the guy.

He looked up. "Just bring yourself."

I flushed. It sounded as if he was reprimanding me.

Fuck you, I said silently. It's me who goes, and you who stays behind.

And that's how I left the Station, so perhaps this is why I didn't notice the Tails they had glued on me, not from *Akkavish* but from *Roshanim*, Itzik's department. The entire road from Tel Aviv, I was clean. But when I actually crossed into Eastern Jerusalem, that's when Itzik's Tailers picked me up.

Afterwards it came out that these were two Yemenites, straight out of *katsa*-course (it was the first year they took Yemenites in, because of the coalition agreement), and someone in the *Q'irya* had the bright idea to provide them with semi-live Op experience by following a 508 agent Across. Because if they could follow a 508 in enemy terrain, undetected (so went the thinking), they were probably good.

Normally this would be true, but this time, they were following me.

I crossed over near the *Me'ah She'arim* quarter, where the Orthodox live, close to the Wailing Wall, where a piece of wire-fence had once been cut and left on a hinge, behind a double row of hanging bedsheets of Rabbi Amram Bloy's Yeshiva.

The hour was perhaps eight, maybe eight-thirty in the evening, and as I emerged into the Eastern part of Jerusalem, the burnoose already on my head (with a green filament in the *aqqal*, to show I was an *Ashraf*, a direct descendant of the prophet Muchammad, for extra respect), the streets were still full, though of course they felt different, with different smells, za'atar, not tzimes, and radios wailing songs of Um Kul'sum, not Yossele Rozenblatt, Abayas on clotheslines, not bedsheets, everything different. Arab different.

I didn't care. I have been Across four times already, and to my surprise I rather liked it. I mean, not the danger, because those who liked that, sooner or later went kack. Me, I just liked the place. The boisterousness of it, the ease, what do I know, maybe also being on my own. I mean, inside Israel, there are always bosses on your back. In the army, in Bible class, in the youth movement, everywhere. Here, I was my own boss. All I had to do was this one little thing, then come back. But in the meantime, the time was mine to kill.

I could have stayed the night in E.J., if I wanted, because usually it's good *Apam* practice to see if you've grown a Tail. And maybe I should have. I could of course take as long as I needed, go anywhere I wanted. A lone 508 on a take-down Across, on his own, nobody tells him what to do, they can't even call him back. The one thing I could not do was go to the Wailing Wall, because the Jordanian *muchabarat* had a permanent stake-out there, to see if anyone came by to look, or seemed to be crying or anything. Benny Gissin himself, the take-down course commander, was once almost caught on a Crossing; and only because he could run so fast (he had been Alliance's champion in the 100-metre-dash, a year before me), did he manage to escape.

38

Anyway, I still don't know why, but I decided to go straight through. Who knows why we decide to do what we do? That's the one thing they can never teach you. Right after you do it, you know it was a mistake. But at the moment it seems right. Maybe many years later you again feel it was right, but a different sort of right. Anyway, I am getting off the story.

So I got into a beat-up cab near the International Hotel, and paid the driver ten dinnars for the trip to Amman, spinning him some story about a wedding in the tribe. (I was going in as a Ta'amra bedouin, who are the kind no-one wants to mess with.) The cabbie nodded to me very equably—both a Ta'amra, and an *Ashraf*, it doesn't go on foot, as they say—and together we waited in silence until the cab filled up—like in Tel Aviv, the cabs always take several passengers on the trip—and we were off.

It took about four hours to get to Amman, because on the way, one of the passengers—a scowling small woman in a black Ababya, with a huge wedding band and a little moustache—got sick, and we had to stop; then there was an accident near Ruj'm, with a motorcycle, and we had to go around it, through the Waq'il road—anyway: to make a long story short, we got to Amman well after midnight.

But now I had a problem, because those days the *shoo-shoo* still didn't have safehouses in Amman, only in Eastern Jerusalem, so I didn't have anyplace to go to. The thing to do, of course, also because I was a bedouin for the duration, was to find a roadside ditch, wrap myself in my Galabieh, and go to sleep there. Maybe even go to a Mosque, they would let me sleep in the yard. But I don't know, sleeping in the ditches I didn't like, because once a snake had crept into my shirt in a Cairo lot, after I had already returned from a job. If there's one thing I hate, it's snakes. Also mosques. That's the other thing I hate, their religion. Such fanatics, if they didn't want to kill us all, maybe we wouldn't have to do this. I mean, Din Muhammad bin

Sayyef—The rule of Mohammad is by the Sword. That's what their Koran says. I am asking you. Is this a way to live?

Anyway. Luckily the other cab riders also had the same problem—we had four men, including me, and two women, the mustachioed one, and an older mama, maybe her relative, or something. The cabbie said he could put us all in different rooms in his brother's house, for fifteen dinnars each. Now, this was plain robbery, but going out on the streets of Amman in '68 after midnight, would have been another kind of robbery. So we all agreed, which for me was the second mistake, because a Ta'amra, even a lazy-bum that doesn't like to sleep in ditches, would have laid his hand on his dagger and said five dinnars. If there's one thing a bedouin is, it's a haggler. But I was tired, so I said okay, and he drove us all to Assafiyeh, which was then a little village North of Amman (today it's a suburb with villas where army officers live), and let us into a large brick house that had once probably been the kuttub, an Islamic school for boys, but which was now broken and derelict like an old urinal. There were mattresses on the floor, and we put them one in each room, and went to sleep after praying each on his own mat.

I then lay down on my mattress, but even though I was tired, I still did the necessary, which means arranging objects around me to make noise if somebody sneaks in on me, like piling one shoe on top of another, balance coins on my tin cigarette case, things like that. And what do you know, about three, four o'clock in the morning, I heard the tinkle of the coins. So, without thinking—we do it twice every night in katzach course—I rolled to the side, and came up with my Bedouin dagger, but by then I already smelled her; it was the small woman, the one with the moustache. She was still in her Abbaya, but now her legs were bare, and her hair was loose. Without saying anything she lay down on my mattress, and looked up at me, and,

40

still saying nothing, began to lift her Abbaya over her head.

The house was totally quiet. No sound at all. Those days, you could be on the outskirts of an Arab town at night and hear quiet like in the desert. Nobody moved. Everybody sleeping, even the jackals. So, also quiet, I lay down beside her, and after a moment raised my Gallabieh also, and then we fucked. It was uncanny, I don't know how to explain it. From the moment we started, we just looked each other in the eye, without saying anything. There was no sound whatsoever, none. And even though it was the most uncomfortable fuck I ever had—both of us were lying on our sides, so she had to lift her leg, and I had to twist my hips, but that's the way we did it—I almost fainted when we finished, so strong it was, my spine felt hollow with the release. Afterwards we just lay there, still not talking, breathing shallowly. She then touched my jaw with lightly callused fingers, and whispered something in my cheek.

"What?" I said.

"Allah shall bless you," she said, to my astonishment, "Ya Ta'amra."

It was then that I made my biggest mistake. I asked her where she was from. She said she was from Amman, and was travelling with her aunt to meet someone—probably her future husband, but I didn't ask; then she asked me where I was from.

"From Ruj'm," I said, like an idiot, because who could tell, maybe she knew people in the refugee camp there.

But she only asked if I was going to be in Amman for long. And like a complete idiot, I said that I would be there only two days.

I couldn't believe myself. A 508 on a take-down, telling his itinerary to a randy Arab bride-to-be. For all I knew, she was part Bedouin too, and then I was as good as dead. With my own prepuce cut off.

But it came out she was just a Palestinian, living with her family in Qarameh from after the '48 Disaster (her family was from Yaffo); and after a few more minutes (she gave me the address of her uncle, in Amman), she got up, towelled herself unselfconsciously with her Abbaya between her legs, and was gone.

Within less than a minute I fell asleep like a dead man, and in the morning, when I got up, everyone was already in the main room, sitting on the dusty floor, eating pita bread and goat cheese and olives with their fingers, and drinking tea. The mustachioed woman and her aunt were seated to the side, both bundled heavily and not looking up.

I don't know, she of course couldn't look at me, because, let's face it, she was with her aunt, and everything. But still. I felt I wanted to see her again, maybe because of the fuck. It was so good, like nothing I ever had. Of course, all I had had till then were short quickies with old whores in Yaffo where all of us from the take-down course used to go on Friday afternoons, I mean those who didn't have families, or girlfriends. But this was somehow, I don't know, different, like as if we were married, or something.

So after I did this Major from the Muchabarrat (it went really smooth, he didn't even wake up, only I threw up a little and had to clean up the place), I stayed behind in Amman like a complete fool, instead of taking the Arava road home, as I've been told, and went to the address she had given me, to see her.

I can hardly believe today what I did. For all I knew, she was already married to some young Palestinian guy, doing his laundry daily, baking his pita bread, sewing his pants. But no, she was there in the yard, cutting some cloth with scissors, and when I peeked through the rails, there she was. So I smiled and passed by quickly; and after a while she came out; and to make a long story short, she told me to get my ass to the Arava road, because they were waiting for me two days already.

I almost fainted right then and there, because who could have guessed they would send a woman after me, the first woman katsach ever, and a Yemenite, too? So when I came back, my defence was that I knew all along she was one of us, but because she was offering, why wouldn't I take?

Gissin said this was bullshit, because if I knew she was one of us, a Yemenite, I wouldn't have taken what she offered, out of decency, because for Yemenite girls, doing it means they can't get married. It's like with the Arabs, for them.

So I said maybe I wanted to marry her myself, and that's why I did it in the first place.

No'a (that was her name) then began to cry (cross my heart), and finally we got married, just to prove to them I knew who she was all along. But of course after three months I left her. Because, fuck it, nobody does this to me. She tried to take me down, I took her.

Darkness

When my Aunt Ofra fell in love with a Yemenite Jew, my mother became sick and did not rise from her bed for a month. But this did not make her sister change her mind, nor the entreaties of her father, my grandfather Moshe Zukerman, who begged her to take pity on him and think of what the neighbours would say. Also to think of her future children, who would be dark-skinned and curly haired and would be destined to hew wood and carry water for white Ashkenazis like us. Finally my grandma Leah weighed in also, with fainting spells—four of them—but nothing helped. My Aunt Ofra was resolved to marry Yiftach, her Yemenite boyfriend whom she had met in the army, where she had served as a clerk for a Paratroop brigade in Sarafend.

This Yiftach, all agreed, even though he was a Yemenite, was rather a nice guy. He had finished high school in Hadera (which was the nearest town to his parents' village)—and in the Mathematical stream, too. Not the first in his class, but still: a Yemenite who can do math is something. He also had a driving licence, and had saved some money working summers as a bookkeeper in a butcher shop in Hadera. This raised his status in the eyes of my father— who had his own butcher shop in Tel Aviv—but not enough to overcome Yiftach's basic deficiency.

"He is a good boy, but we never had a Yemenite in the family," my father said, "and I hope we never will."

There were also all sorts of snide remarks about the real reason Ofra had set her heart on Yiftach. Everyone knew about Yemenites, who gave their wives children even when they were 90 years old. Some said it was because of the hot pepper they ate, others said it was because their ancestors' blood had mixed with Arabs', during the many generations that they have lived in Yemen, and everyone knew about Arabs.

Not that anyone suspected that Ofra had any such matters with Yiftach. In those days women waited until they got married. But tongues wagged.

Even so, Ofra would not change her mind. She even threatened to marry Yiftach in his Yemenite village, in front of his relatives only, without her own family attending. By that time, my mother finally decided to take matters in hand, and one day she took bus No. 25 and travelled to the edge of King George Street, and from there, on foot, to the Yemenites' quarter at the edge of the Carmel market.

I was then seven years old. It was the summer holidays, mid August, and my mother, having no place to leave me, took me with her.

"But you'd better forget anything you see or hear, or you'll get it from your father, you hear?"

I nodded, though I could not see what was so secret about going to the Yemenites' quarter. I had visited it with my mother several times before. Yemima, our erstwhile cleaner, lived there with her family, in a shack in the midst of a yard surrounded by a stone wall. Even after Yemima had stopped cleaning for us, from time to time my mother visited her to buy lufa, which grew on the shack's wall in great profusion, or mint leaves, or brown eggs laid by chickens that ran inside the enclosed yard.

But this time it was not for lufa or eggs that my mother had come to see Yemima, and our old cleaner seemed to know it. She greeted us dressed in a wide black dress under which she wore the traditional striped pants of the Yemenite woman, and gave me a salt-biscuit to munch on while she and my mother discussed the case of my Aunt Ofra.

"It won't end well," my mother finished. "But we don't know what to do."

If I had expected Yemima to defend Yiftach, or Ofra (whom she knew since Ofra was a girl), I was disappointed. Yemima, like my mother, seemed to disapprove of the entire affair. "She's not for him," Yemima agreed, who

45

knew Yiftach also. "He wants to go to University, what does he need a wife so early?"

This seemed to nettle my mother, but did not deflect her from her goal. "I don't know what to do," she repeated. "Maybe something? You know, you have anything?"

Yemima seemed to hesitate. Finally she got up. "Wait here," she said.

Through the window I could see her rummaging among the weeds in the yard, shooing away chickens. While she was out, my mother sat stiff and unmoving, looking straight ahead. I had finished my salt cookie and did not have anything to do besides counting the silver benediction cups in the cupboard. (There were twelve.) Once or twice I thought of asking my mother a question, but reconsidered. At last Yemima came back. In her fist were a few sprigs of a dark green weed. She put them all on the table before her, where they seemed to exude a faint musk.

"This is not for money, you understand," she said.

My mother said she was willing to pay. But Yemima's eyes blackened. "No, no. This is not for money."

My mother's face stiffened. "All right. Not for money."

From her apron's pocket Yemima produced an air-mail writing pad, tore out a flimsy lined sheet, and wrapped it around the dark weeds. "Here. In tea, not in coffee."

My mother stuck the wrapped weeds in her pocket, got up, and we left.

On the way home my mother was silent. Once again I tried to ask her about the meaning of all this, but became frightened into silence.

At home my father was waiting. He often came home for lunch at summer. He and my mother chased me out, to play with other kids by the mulberry tree, and they closeted themselves in the living-room.

When I came home in the evening, I looked all over the house to see where the sheaf of weeds was hidden. I found it behind the Passover plates. A day later my Aunt Ofra came to visit—without Yiftach, who was on guard duty at the base. She had tea and cake with my parents. After she had left I rushed to the kitchen to see if the weeds were still there. They were, still wrapped in the flimsy air-mail paper.

Over the next several months, my aunt came to visit several more times, once or twice with Yiftach, who in the meantime had finished his military service and was applying to the Technion, to study Electrical Engineering. Ofra was evidently very much smitten with him; he was affectionate and polite.

Every time after their visit, I would rush to see whether the weeds had been put to use. After six months they were still there. Whether because my mother could not bring herself to do it, or had simply reconsidered, I could not tell.

Then Yiftach started his studies in the Technion. My Aunt Ofra applied to Haifa University, to study sociology and liberal arts, but was not accepted. She came in one or two points below the threshold, my mother said. One or two points! Couldn't they make an exception for such a talented girl? Ofra then travelled to Haifa in person to explain she wanted to be near her boyfriend. But nothing helped. So she went to work for a bank in Tel Aviv as a clerk, and for a few months Yiftach, who had taken a room in Haifa, travelled weekly to Tel Aviv to see her on weekends. But after a while, as his study schedule became heavier, his visits became sparser; and when he did come, he and Ofra seemed to have less and less to talk about. Finally, his visits stopped altogether, and a year or so later I heard he was getting married to a girl who studied Aeronautical Engineering whom he met in some class.

"An Ashkenazi?" my mother asked, when I told her.

I said I thought Yiftach's wife was from Be'er Sheva.

"But her parents?"

I said I heard they were Bulgarian Jews, or perhaps Rumanian.

"Hah. I betcha they're Moroccan," my father said.

"Blackies like him."

My mother said nothing. Somehow I didn't think the news gave her as much comfort as it did my father.

After a while my Aunt Ofra began to go out with Hezkel, the butcher at my father's Ibn Gabirol store (by that time my father had three stores), and she finally married him.

By and by I forgot about the weeds in the kitchen cupboard. But one day, when I was already in the army myself (this was twelve years later), and I came home for Passover on a furlough, my mother asked me to take down the Passover dishes, from the cupboard over the fridge. As I was picking up the white porcelain tureen, I saw the old packet lying on its side behind it, its contents dry and crumbling.

I asked my mother why she had not thrown it away.

"Thrown away what?" she said.

When I explained, she pretended she did not know what I was talking about.

"From Yemima," I said. "Remember?"

My mother became very cross, and chased me out of her kitchen. She had to cook for lots of guests, she said, and needed no pesky helpers.

Later that day, just before the Seder itself, I peeked into the cupboard, fully expecting the packet to be gone. But it was still there, lying on its side, undisturbed.

Later still, in the Seder, the conversation somehow turned to our old cleaning lady. I don't know who brought up her name. Perhaps I did.

"She died three years ago," my father said. "I don't know from what."

"Heart attack," my mother said. "I went to her funeral. You were busy with the second store."

"And the Yemenite boy," I said, "the one who used to go out with Ofra, what became of him?"

No-one seemed to know. But then Ofra volunteered that he was now a professor in America. "He emigrated," she said. "Without any shame."

"I'll never leave Israel," her husband, Hezkel, said. "What do we lack here? Nothing." He asked for more gefilte fish and finished it all, including the bones, which he crunched between his healthy white teeth.

That same year, Ofra, to everyone's surprise, began to study Hebrew Literature in Tel Aviv University. Because the butcher shop was doing well, there was no need for her to work anymore, and so she stopped working in the bank, prepared well for the entrance exam and managed to pass. She then hired a Yemenite cleaning lady that also took the two boys to and from school, and Ofra herself dedicated her time to her books. It took two years—an unheard of short time—for Ofra to get her B.A. Then she did nothing with it. But during the Passover Seder following her graduation, she announced in a low voice that Hezkel and she were going to be divorced. Her two children sat with their heads low. They did not cry—for them it must have been known already.

"But why?" my father shouted. "You found someone else?"

Ofra shook her head.

"Hezkel is not a good husband? You don't love him anymore?"

Ofra took Hezkel's hand and said he was a good husband.

"So why?"

To everyone's surprise, Ofra began to cry. "Because I have to. I have other things."

The following week Ofra took a room above a grocery store in the Carmel Market, and began writing the first of her books. The following year she came to our house for the Seder—Hezkel and the boys came too. After the Seder I rushed to the kitchen cupboard to look for the weed packet. But it was of course gone.

49

Dybbuk

Avraham Schlein was sitting at the Yeshiva's window, when he chanced to raise his eyes from the Talmud's page of Uncleanliness Laws he had been studying. Out in Carmi Street, a black motorcycle was racing toward the orange light. As a white car swept into view, cutting the motorcycle off, Avraham half rose from his seat. But before he could get up fully, the motorcycle had already been swallowed by the car's wheels. Only then did the screech of the brakes and the shouts reach him. It was just after eleven o'clock.

He ran down the steps and into the street, pushing past the crowd of other Yeshiva boys, bearded instructors and visiting fathers. A policeman with a red welt on his neck was reclining over the limp figure of a man in army fatigues. The man did not have a helmet. Presently an ambulance arrived, gathered the limp body and departed.

For a few minutes the Yeshiva boys milled about, breathing in the excitement, then, one by one, went back to their studies. Avraham, too, went back in.

Next day his brother Chayim came to visit. Chayim was a clerk in the central T'nuva store, in Natanya, helping their father support Avraham's studies. Avraham took Chayim to see the scene of the accident.

"Here?" said Chayim, bending over the road.

"Yes," said Avraham. The small pool of blood on the asphalt was congealed by now. "Right here."

"And you saw it?"

"Yes, everything." Feeling an odd thrill, Avraham stepped on the dry stain, mashing it around with his sandal.

That night, Avraham's brother stayed to sleep in one of the small guest-rooms. Next day, Avraham's father, a municipal employee in Bney Barak's water department, also came to visit, and that afternoon Avraham and his brother accompanied him to Beit Dayan cemetery, to lay a pebble on their mother's headstone.

The day was overcast, the sky low. A funeral was taking place not far off. A group of girl-soldiers stood by an open grave, crying and chattering in whispers. One, a tall brown-haired girl, smiled tenderly at Avraham. His right toe itched fiercely and he bent over to scratch it, through the sandal. When he rose he saw the girl was still looking at him. Confused, he stared back, scowling. But to his consternation she came over, hesitantly, and asked if he was with the Yeshiva.

Avraham's father and brother had gone off to look at the grave of an uncle, near the fence. Avraham was all alone.

"Yes," he said, his heart hammering like a loose stone.

She went on, "Who—who did you come to bury?" She seemed surprised at her own audacity.

"N...no-one." Briefly he explained about the year-day, and the kaddish-prayer duty. But before he was half-way through, she interrupted him.

"I—I came for a funeral," she said. "My boyfriend died, in an accident—"

He tried to keep his eyes on the ground, as proper, but found them rising of their own accord. In a low voice he said he was sorry.

There was a pause. In the distance, he could see his father and brother swaying over a tombstone.

He raised his eyes fully and looked at her. She stared right back at him. The moment lengthened.

"What's your name?" she asked.

He told her. Her eyes were large and brown, and her nose straight.

"Mine is Deena," she said, blushing deep red.

There was another pause.

Impulsively, she pulled a Dubek cigarette box out of her handbag, tore its back off and wrote down a phone number, rapidly. "I...I don't know why I am doing this—"

He mumbled something, grabbed the cardboard, and escaped.

Back at the Yeshiva, his father and brother already gone, the image of the girl did not leave him. The following evening, after ceaseless self-torment, he called her from the grocery store across the street.

They talked for a few minutes, hesitantly, about nothing. "I—I have to go," he said at last. One of the instructors had just come in, and was turning over a long herring, inside the wooden barrel, with a nicotine-stained finger. "I—I don't know if I can call—"

"So write to me," she said.

When he said nothing, she recited her address, and he let it rise before his eyes in sharp letters of fire, as he did with Talmud phrases, to memorize them.

"So you'll write?" she asked.

"Y...yes."

Next day he did, enclosing his picture from the year-end photograph of his *Chavurah* in that trip to the Gallil, his hat jammed down over his head, like a helmet.

He posted the letter in the evening, at the mailbox near the bus station, when no-one was watching, then ran back to his studies. (Again he had failed Divorces, and had to go for review before the chief tutor. It was hard going.)

Later that week he received a letter back, with her picture. She was wearing a yellow bikini, and was sitting on a black rock in some beach, a bird pecking at the sand behind her, just over her naked shoulder.

Avraham stared at the picture for a long hour, transfixed. He paled at the thought of what might have happened if the Chief Instructor had opened the letter. Usually he opened all. This time he didn't.

The following week was exam week. Avraham passed

Divorces, Uncleanliness and Egg, but had to re-study for Deprivations. On Thursday afternoon, instead of memorizing the 49 Unclean Gates, he went out to meet Deena.

They met in the Machaneh Yehuda suk, in the midst of the jumble of vegetable stalls, falafel vendors, and crowds of Arabs and Jews. She wore a short bleached khaki skirt and a pink T-shirt; he had taken off his hat and had folded up the sleeves of his white shirt. The small-shawl's fringes he had stuck into his pants, inside.

"You look just like someone," she said, blinking, "But I can't remember who." Her face glowed reddish pink in the sun, the wind whisking her brown hair around her ears. She smelled of soap and mothballs. "Doesn't matter."

Later they ate hummus and taheena from one plate, wiping the goo with two pittas, together. Then they drank two raspberry *gazozs* and, at Deena's suggestion, went in to cinema Sheffer. It was the first movie Avraham had ever seen. It was as vivid as the Talmud. Deena made him sit at the far back, and as the movie started, she grabbed his head and kissed him on the side of his mouth.

"I can't stop thinking of you," she whispered.

On the screen, Audrey Hepburn and Cary Grant cavorted and danced. But Deena looked only at him.

Stuttering, Avraham whispered he could not stop thinking of her either. He turned his head, and, heart frozen with fear, let her kiss him fully, her lips smearing against his. Her breath smelled of oil and hummus, and a faint tang of earth.

"I live in Rehavia," she said. "Maybe you can come to visit?"

Rehavia was the poshest neighbourhood of Jerusalem. He had never been there before.

"All right." He nodded, shakily.

But that night when he returned to the Yeshiva, he learned someone had seen him in the Cinema and reported it. The following day his father arrived from Bney Barak.

53

"If you want your son to remain here," said Rabbi Kleinman, cleaning under his fingernails with an open scissors blade, "do something."

They were seated in the Rabbi's office, under a photograph of the Chazon Ish, the photo's eyes bitter and severe, the eyebrows joined, the beard forked.

"I—I want him to finish," said Avraham's father. "To be a Rabbi." He began to weep. "My wife, may she rest in peace, wanted it too."

"So tell him," said Rabbi Kleinman. "We have rules here. Very strict. Comes a Gvir, wants us to find a Shiduch for his daughter, a studious good boy, what do you want I should say? That he's been going out with some nafka? Or maybe I should lie, say no?"

Avraham's father cried some more. Avraham had never seen his father cry like that. He, too, wept now, and said he could not stop thinking of the girl. "She...she is burning in my mind!" he stammered, grief-stricken. "I—I can't—even when I am in the toilet—"

"Shah! Avreimel!" cried his father. "What are you saying?!"

"I can't!" Avraham cried back. "It's burning—"

Avraham's father said that maybe the boy couldn't help it. "It hap...happens," he stammered, "sometimes, n...not from his own fault—"

The Rabbi spit three times, quickly.

"Yes," Avraham's father said. "It happens—"

There was a short silence. Only Avraham's sobs could be heard. Presently Rabbi Kleinman closed the scissors, with a click. "Listen, Mr. Schlein, you want, I'll give you a few names," he muttered. He tore a piece of HaTzofeh newspaper, and wrote on it. "With experience."

The pause turned brittle.

"But you didn't hear it from me," Rabbi Kleinman went on, looking out the window as Avraham's father put the paper in his vest pocket.

"No, never!" Avraham's father said. "May God repay you 77 times!"

"Nu, go, go," said Rabbi Kleinman. "Before I change my mind."

The first exorcist they saw lived in the Yamin Moshe neighbourhood, over a bicycle shop, a Moroccan lay Rabbi by the name of Zevulun Ben Hammo.

His wife opened the door. She was a tall woman with a grey moustache, and walked with a limp.

"Four thousand had consulting me," said Rabbi Ben Hammo, a corpulent balding man with a thick beard, "about dybbuks, and evil spirits."

"Also barren wives and missing husbands," added his wife.

"Sometimes," said Ben Hammo modestly. He pointed to a broom closet. "To get undressed there, please. Also the underwear."

Inside the closet, Avraham took off his clothes slowly. When he came out, he saw to his consternation that the Rabbi's wife had remained. She was sprinkling some yellow liquid into the four corners of the room, from a Tempo bottle.

"They hate the smell," her husband explained. "Into a woman they get through the cunt, begging your pardon, into a man from the ass, also begging your pardon, so they don't like to be reminded."

Avraham's father sat hunched in a small chair, hands clasped between his knees. Avraham, his right foot itching, stood shivering in the middle of the room, covering his genitals with two hands.

"Not to be afraid," said Rabbi Ben Hammo. Without warning, he stuck a metallic bathroom hose into Avraham's ear, and in a high pitched voice, began declaiming incantations in Aramaic, frequently shouting, "Out! Out, you unclean spirit!"

After five minutes of shouting, he began to cough, loudly and pointedly.

"Always," Rabbi Ben Hammo's wife said. "He can smell them, immediately. Like burnt rubber, they smell, the Others."

Avraham tried to nod; but at that moment Rabbi Ben Hammo grabbed his earlobe. "Out!" hollered the Rabbi. "Out!" He bent over Avraham and bit the ear between his front teeth.

Avraham slumped over, nearly fainting from the pain. Rabbi Ben Hammo led him to a chair, and Avraham sat down. Then, not knowing how or why, he felt himself drifting to sleep.

"Let him," he heard Rabbi Ben Hammo say.

A few minutes later Avraham felt himself waking up. Confused, he put on his clothes.

"Two hundred and fifty shekel," said the Rabbi's wife.

Avraham's father, face wet with tears and perspiration, counted out the money. The Rabbi's wife went to the kitchen, to make change for a 100-shekel bill. When she came back, she handed Avraham and his father a sliver of a M'lawach, a Yemenite salt cookie.

"Eat, it's good after," she said.

Outside, Avraham threw his into some bushes. His father ate his.

In the cab, Avraham's father said, "So?"

Avraham said, "I—I still want to see her—"

There was a pause.

"Nu," said his father. "So we'll go to another one."

The following month, Avraham stayed at his father's apartment in Bney Barak, sneaking out occasionally to call Deena, while his father took him to three more exorcists. A Yemenite woman in Kerem HaTeymanim, who laid him down naked inside a shallow square pit, in which she had burnt Hadass leaves and unknown spices the night before; a

75-year-old Kabbalist in Safed, whose emaciated body shook in his black Kapota, as he danced around Avraham, holding unlit black candles; and finally, a twenty-year-old Moroccan girl named Sarina, of whom Avraham's father had heard independently in the Carmel market, while buying brisket.

The girl had fair hair and black eyes, and smelled of lemon and soap. She lived above a butcher shop that belonged to her father. Her father was an Ashkenazi, her mother a Moroccan.

"She got it from her grandmother, my side," the butcher's wife said to Avraham's father, as he and Avraham stood before her in the shop, hats in hand. "She just started last year, but she's good, listen to me. Two dybbuks she had chased already, from soldiers who came back from Lebanon, little Arab children that got—"

"This one we don't know who it is," Avraham's father said.

"I know," said Avraham.

"No you don't," said his father. "Shah."

"Doesn't matter," the exorcist's mother said. "Come."

She locked the front door, opened a door at the back, and climbed the stairs, with Avraham's father, and Avraham, following.

The exorcist's room was on the roof, a converted laundry nook. A poster of Chava Albershtein playing her guitar hung on the wall; underneath it, on the bed, was a pink worn-out doll in a black dress; red velvet cushions lay on the floor, here and there, on the chairs and under the low plywood table. White candle-stubs were stuck to the table's surface, burnt down to their wicks.

When they entered, the girl, tall and lanky in a loose red dress, was bending over the table, lighting yet one more candle. As she straightened, she spit on the match, expertly.

She was no more than twenty, Avraham saw, her hair tied in two braids, which fell down her back, trailing black

57

ribbons. Her feet were small, and were shod in red pumps. But her ankles were thick.

"Lie down, here," she said. "And you," she addressed Avraham's father in formal tones, "please to go out."

Walking sideways, Avraham's father left, blinking forlornly.

Avraham, his heart bumping against his ribs, lay down on the mattress, on the floor. Before the door had even closed, without much ado, the girl took off the dress over her head, and lay, supple, next to him, then looked him in the eye. Avraham dared not look down; whether she wore a brassiere, or an undershirt, he could not tell. But he could feel her body exuding heat, from her toes to her head.

His foot twitched and buzzed, as if grilled from the inside. He felt weak with nameless emotion.

"WHO ARE YOU?" the girl rumbled.

Avraham felt himself going faint.

"Me?" he asked. His voice was not his own.

The girl opened her eyes wide; they were nearly all pupil. "Go to your rest," she said. "You had your time, now it is his!" In a different voice she said, "He misses her, and cannot leave. I must make him see she is not the only one." Spreading her lips, she implanted an open kiss on Avraham's mouth, her own lips hot and wet and rubbery. Her tongue probed his, long and tasting of almonds. He felt hands under his belt, then below it.

"Shhhh," she said.

After a while he heard himself shout out loud.

From outside came his father's voice, muffled. "Are you all right, Avreimele?"

"Y...yes," he said, his voice again his own.

The heat had dissipated, and had turned into warmth.

"Shh," said Sarina. "It is necessary. Shhh."

Half an hour later he came out. His father looked at him for a moment, then took out his wallet and began to count money.

"No," said Sarina. "Give to charity." She held her hand high; Avraham's father kissed it, on the palm.

"Not necessary," she said; but did not withdraw the hand.

Avraham wanted to kiss her palm too, but did not dare.

On the way out his father said, "It's out, finally?"

"Yes," said Avraham. "For sure."

He looked over his shoulder. Sarina was standing in the window. She smiled at him.

Paper Bride

In 1934 my Aunt Nechama in Tel Aviv received a letter from her sister Chaya in Warsaw in which Chaya, an actress with the Yiddish Theatre, threatened to kill herself because, due to their father's lack of money, she could not find a *Shiduch*, a Jewish match. As an unmarried girl, and a theatre actress to boot, the Polish goyim were of course after her, and, as Chaya said in her letter, some of them, though anti-Semites, were very handsome; so how long could she hold off? Her only recourse was Palestine, where even a girl without a dowry could get a Jewish husband, just like my Aunt Nechama did.

The problem was, this was right after Ernest Bevan had published the White Paper on Palestine, and so the British, who ruled Palestine then, did not give out many Immigration Certificates. Even men had trouble getting them. As for women, only married ones could get in. So many young Jews from Palestine grabbed their chance, took the boat to Poland, and for good money (evil tongues say for other things also) made fictitious marriages with poor desperate Jewish girls who had nothing, and wanted to leave Poland no matter how. A paper marriage cost less than a ticket to America, and certainly less than a dowry. Chaya, though, did not have even that, so poor her father was. So my Aunt Nechama's heart broke for her sister's suffering, and also from fear that, to get out, Chaya would pay the other kind of payment. So, to make a long story short, after a while Nechama suggested to her own husband (that's my uncle Meshulam Tartakover, the dramatic actor and the brother of the great Yiddish writer G.S. Tartakover) that they divorce, and he, Meshulam, go to Warsaw and marry her sister, on paper. Then he could bring Chaya to Palestine, all legal, and divorce her and get married again with her, Nechama, his wife.

If it all sounds crazy and complicated, let me tell you, others did that, too. Either Jewish girls came to Palestine on a tourist visa, then got married fictitiously in the Rabbinate, and after three years (when they got their citizenship) got a Gett; or, like I said, good boys from Palestine went to Poland (or Russia, or Rumania), and got married there on paper, to get the girls out. Rabbis everywhere played along, and made the weddings crooked on purpose. Like telling the groom to say to the bride, "Thou are not sanctified to me," or not give her the ring, or write the wrong words in the Ktuba, the marriage certificate. Then the Gett would be easy—and this was necessary, because some unscrupulous boys did not want to give the women a divorce later, or, before they finally did, they first asked for money, or worse. So it was necessary to do it crooked from the beginning.

Anyway, to go back to the story, what my Aunt Nechama planned, took place. First my Uncle Meshulam divorced her (there was even a little party afterwards, at the back of Café Cassit, where my uncle invited half the actors of HaBima, to celebrate), and next day, with my aunt's blessing and a package of kosher food for the road, he took an Italian boat from Yaffo to Firenze, and from there, a third-class train to Warsaw.

Now this was already the end of 1934, so Europe was not the best place for a Jew to travel, and especially not to sleep in hotels. So everywhere he passed, Meshulam either slept on his bags, like a wanderer, or at the homes of Yiddish theatre actors, of whom (this was 1934) there were thousands. Finally, when he came to Warsaw, since he was the brother of G.S. Tartakover, everyone, not just Yiddish actors, wanted to take him in to hear about his famous brother in America.

At first Meshulam was a bit offended by this—not that he was such a big fish in the Hebrew theatre, like Buchman, or Kagan, but still. He did play King Achashverosh once, in *Esther's Dream*, and was understudy for Katchalski himself in *King Lear*. But on the road, as they say, even a Rabbi eats leftovers, and being brother to an American author is better than nothing. So, because he was in such hot demand all of a sudden, Meshulam stayed a whole month in Warsaw, not just with theatre actors, but also with hoity toity literature buffs, and only finally with Chaya's and Nechama's father (that's my grandfather Menachem-Leib Zussman), who was only a tailor, and so worked at home and could have a man-guest without evil tongues wagging, even if everyone knew it was only for the Certificate.

So, at the end of the month Meshulam and Chaya were married by Rabbi Yechezkel-Zalman Tuvim, chief Rabbi of Warsaw; and, after saying goodbye to all the Yiddish actors he had met, and to the literary hoi poloi, Meshulam took his young paper bride on the train to Firenze, and from there, in a Greek boat, to Yaffo.

At that time, if I figure correctly (this was already 1935), Meshulam was 42 years old, and Chaya (my mother), maybe 23. Even though he had been in her father's house almost two weeks, this was the first time they could really talk: at her home, there was always her father, or her mother, or some aunt or uncle, with them, to make it proper, so no tongue could wag. Only on the boat could they finally start talking about theatre, and about acting (what else?), and after a while it came out Chaya had always wanted to play something in Hebrew, too (which she knew, because her father was a good Zionist), but who would give her a chance? So Meshulam, wanting to show off, promised to introduce her to Baruch Gissin, who in those days was like a God in Tel Aviv's bohema circles, because of his theatre *HaMakkel*, the Stick; and also because, together with Efraim Tzemer, he, Gissin, ran an actors' school in Yaffo where Riva Yellin herself taught, and sometimes also Re'uven Kagan, and Emil Shaposhnikov, who had all trained with Stanislavsky in Moscow, and after he died, with his disciple Vachtangov. And this Gissin, Meshulam said, was his best friend (which was a lie), and would give her, Chaya, a good role immediately, if he, Meshulam, only asked him. What Meshulam demanded from her, in exchange for this opportunity, is a subject for debate. To this day Meshulam says, only a kiss. Chaya says, he asked for more, and also promised more than just a role; and from this all the trouble started. But let me tell it in order.

After nine days at sea, the boat arrived in Yaffo (on 23 January, 1935), and Meshulam and Chaya went ashore in a little dinghy (which everyone had to take, since the big boat could not dock in the shallow harbour). My Aunt Nechama was already waiting, on pins, as they say, and saw them get off hand in hand (—in case the British were watching, Meshulam said later). She ran toward them, but the British gappir barred her way: it came out there had been an outbreak of Scarlatina in Europe, so everyone who came from there had to stay in quarantine, until the British army doctor came from Sarafend to check them, to see if maybe they were sick.

Did they have a choice? No. So, with Nechama wailing behind, Meshulam and Chaya went to the Pension Globerman, in Jabbeliyah, which in those days was the quarantine for immigrants without papers, or with some disease, and they stayed there a whole week—and in the same room, so the British wouldn't get suspicious—before the doctor came and pronounced everyone healthy, and let them go. And during that week, like you probably guessed, they read plays, in Yiddish and Hebrew, and also fell in love.

Now, it was a problem, but not like you think. Because Meshulam, although an actor, was also an honourable man, and he says he never touched Chaya like a husband. Go learn the truth, but me, I believe him. You only had to hear him recite *Hamlet* once, to realize this was not a man who would make up his mind to do anything like this in a month. The problem was the reverse: it was Chaya now who did not want a Gett. Sure, the wedding in Warsaw had been fake, and the ktuba had five mistakes in it, on purpose, like I said. But during the boat trip the Ktuba somehow had been lost (later it came out that Chaya threw it into the sea), so paper-marriage or not, all of a sudden Meshulam had to have a real Gett, and Chaya did not want to give it.

Now, as you probably know, if a Jew refuses to give his wife a Gett, it's a problem, because only a hundred Rabbis, who all agree together, can annul the marriage. On the other hand, if the wife refuses, a simple Rabbinical court, a Beit Din, can give the husband a Gett on her behalf, and she can say nothing. So at first it seemed there would be no problem, especially with the crooked wedding, the "Thou are not sanctified to me," and everything. Until Chaya said that all this was immaterial, because Meshulam really did touch her like a husband, which she agreed to, because, first, he promised her a role in Gissin's theatre—any role she wanted; and second, he also promised to stay married to her. And because he had promised this, she said, it superseded everything else: the errors in the ktuba, the mistakes in the wedding's utterance, all the crookedness.

Meshulam, for his part, insisted he promised nothing, only once, on deck, when he got carried away by the moon and some scenes of a play they were reciting, from Shakespeare, and only for a kiss; but immediately afterwards he asked Chaya her forgiveness, which she gave. As for the role, he said he had explained it was only a maybe, nothing was for sure. And regarding the forgiveness, he insisted that Chaya had forgiven him everything, but he refused to give details.

But Chaya said it wasn't like this at all. She denied she gave him any forgiveness whatsoever, neither for the kiss, nor for the trickery with the role, or for anything else, so his promise to stay married held.

My Aunt Nechama, who was then already living again with my Uncle Meshulam, but who wanted to be his wife also, was at her wits' end. There were big fights, with lots of screaming, and tearing of hair, and also late-night scenes at Café Cassit, after the shows (my Aunt Nechama was then playing Leahleh, in the Dybbuk), with some actors taking Meshulam's side, others Chaya's, others still saying they didn't believe any of them. Finally it went all the way to Rabbi Blau, who was then the chief Rabbi of Tel Aviv (and today is the Israeli chief Ashkenazi Rabbi), and who, after hearing everybody together and each one separately, said that unfortunately Chaya was correct, and that by the Hallacha, Jewish law, she had to be given the benefit of the doubt; so Meshulam's promise was a promise until she forgave it.

So now this became a real tragedy, because, first, my Aunt Nechama, who had done all this just to save her sister from the anti-Semites in Poland and from the shame of no husband, now had no husband herself, even if they were living together; and if she were to kick him out—which some said she should do—who would marry her, the ex-wife of a man married to another, on-paper? And second, to add to the complication, Meshulam had really fallen in love with Chaya, like I said, and even though he kept saying he wanted to divorce her and re-marry Nechama, because this was the honourable thing to do, whenever Chaya came to him crying, his heart melted, and straightaway he went back to her to the rooms she was then renting, over Starkman's shoe-store on Herzl Street. Now, whether he touched her then like a husband or not, I don't know, and don't want to know. Why add to my aunt's troubles, bringing it all up again.

Anyway, finally finally in 1937, after this was going on for maybe three years, Baruch Gissin decided to stage *A Midsummer Night's Dream*, in Hebrew, which Micha Cohen-Kadosh (Kadishevitz) had just translated from the Polish translation, and the poet Avraham Shlonsky himself had pronounced better than the original.

As you can imagine, the competition for the roles was fierce. I've heard it said that some actresses offered themselves to Gissin (who of course had no interest, being at the time Paltiel Rubin's boyfriend), and to Tzemer (who partook, but then did nothing for them), and two of these (from Haifa) swallowed Iodine, when they were not chosen. But maybe it's just one more of Cassit's tall-tales. Who knows. What is sure is that the role of Titania was especially prized, since it was rumoured that G.S. Tartakover himself would come from America to see the show, and would maybe recommend the actress for a Yiddish movie he was then planning, with Samuel Goldwyn, on the same topic. So, true or not, all of Tel Aviv was on wheels, as they say. For a whole month Gissin had daily auditions, in his studio in Yaffo, with people standing at the windows half the night to catch a glimpse of the actors, as they came to try out their luck in the morning. Riva Yellin herself tried, and failed. (She, too, took Iodine.) Then Sonya Bukovsky, and also Pnina Tzurin, and Tova Fein—in short, everyone, except my aunt, Nechama Tartakover, who, though she was dying to play Titania, said she would leave this to her sister, so that she, Chaya, would give her back her husband. But Chaya would not audition, on principle.

"He promised to get me any role I wanted," she said, meaning Meshulam, "so now I don't have to."

Gissin of course did not even want to talk to her, because

first, who was Meshulam Tartakover to promise anything in his, Gissin's, name? And second, with all the actresses running after him, Gissin, (even though he had no interest), what did he have to run after a Yiddish actress with no experience for?

The problem was, after three weeks of auditions, Gissin still had not found his Titania. He had auditioned maybe 50 actresses (and Tzemer, perhaps twenty more), but none fitted. She had to be exactly right, Gissin said, or no play. So, finally, taking his honour in his hands, as they say, he went to my Aunt Nechama, and beseeched her to come to the auditions also. At first she refused, like I said; but after he talked to her maybe two days (Meshulam talked, too), she finally agreed.

Now, let me tell you, this was really something. Even Uzi Kaizer's book ("Hebrew Theatre, Whence and Wherefore," Volume II), which doesn't always go into details, even it tells how half Tel Aviv came to watch Nechama's audition. And what didn't she read? She read everything. Parts of Manger's *Megilla*; and scenes from *Romeo and Juliet*, in Polish (translation of Miczkewitz); and also Bialik poems, and Tchernichovsky sonnets; and finally also parts from *A Midsummer Night's Dream*, at least three roles. It took a whole day. Only she auditioned; no-one else. Finally, in the evening, both Gissin and Tzemer took her to the back room, and there, quietly, they told her she had not been chosen, because somehow something was missing. So, without saying anything, Nechama right away went home and took Iodine also; but because Meshulam was ready, he took her to Hadassah hospital, and they saved her life.

But now listen to this: that very same night, with Nechama still in Hadassah, Chaya went up to Gissin, in Café Cassit, stood with her hands on her hips before him and said, for everyone to hear, "Now that you didn't take her, if you give it to me, I will give him the Gett." Just like that.

Gissin later said he at first thought Chaya was joking. But then, when she repeated it, he realized she meant it. So he said to her, "First you give Shulem," (that's what they called my uncle), "the Gett, like you should, then you'll get it."

"On your word?" she said.

And Gissin replied, "Before everybody here, yes."

So next day, with Nechama still in hospital, Chaya and Meshulam went to Rabbi Blau, and he divorced them properly. All the actors of Tel Aviv came to see it—only this time there was no party afterwards; instead, when they had finished signing, Chaya wanted to go to Yaffo, to start on the rehearsals (every other role had already been filled), but Gissin took her and all the other actors to Café Cassit, and, there, before everyone, he said to her, "My promise to you is as good as your first promise to him to divorce, after all he had done for you, and had saved your life."

Chaya fainted, and after she was woken up with ammonia from Cassit's kitchen, Gissin said, again for all to hear, "This *nafka*, if she wants it, she has to audition for it just like everyone else."

What can I say? It was a sensation. The British High Commissioner himself, George McMichael, who had heard about this from the CID spies, called Gissin in secret and said his own wife wanted to learn as a favour if this was true. Then Rabbi Blau called, and said if he, Rabbi Blau, had known this was going to happen, he wouldn't have done the divorce, because a wife has rights also. And I am told that Golda Meirson also called, but whether to congratulate Gissin or to scold him, I don't know. Anyway, all this was of course too late, because, unlike the paper-wedding, the divorce was good and kosher.

Now, to finish with the story: for all of the following week Tel Aviv was in uproar. Half of the bohema applauded Gissin, the other half said he was as bad as she was. And to make it really worse, a few days later Chaya herself took Laudanum, which is like Iodine, only worse, and when Nechama found her sister half-dead, when she came to visit (Meshulam, who had in the meantime remarried Nechama, no longer did), she had to call a taxi and take Chaya to Hadassah hospital, where the doctors pumped her stomach, too, and saved her life also.

So, to really cut the story short (because what do the details matter?), Chaya did try out finally for the role of Titania, on the very last day (Jewish actresses were already coming from America, to audition), and she got it. And now the evil tongues really started wagging, because (so they said), after all this tall-tale, how could Gissin not give her the role? Just to see this *tzatzke* as the queen of feys, and also Meshulam, for whom she had done all this, who wouldn't buy a ticket? And that's exactly how it happened. Although G.S. Tartakover never came, the show was a great success— so much so that Gissin even toured America with it, for three weeks.

So why am I telling you all this? Because in the play, Chaya finally fell out of love with Meshulam (who had played Puck), and fell into love with Pinchas Cherniak, a pioneer from G'dera who played theatre on the side, (he was Bottom), and she married him, and after eight months I was born, so maybe some good did come out of all this. But after three months (before I was even born) they (Chaya and Cherniak) divorced (he died eight years later, in the Castel battle), and today she is in America, married (as I am sure you know) to G.S. Tartakover, whom she had met during the tour, and is living in Florida, and still appearing in the Yiddish Theatre in Tampa, even at her age, which is already more than 70.

Several times she wrote to me, after my own plays began to appear, in Tel Aviv, but I never even opened her letters. Why bother? As my Uncle Meshulam used to say, you can never trust actors, because no matter what they say, first, they lie to keep in practice, and second, it's only a paper role they are playing, even in life, and they'd do anything to get another, if they think it's better.

Og

The Elders came for him late at night, before dawn, just like last time. Og didn't know how he knew that, but the knowledge arrived upon him even before the dank rot inside the casket turned fresher in his nostrils and the nerve-jangling creak of the sliding lid rattled his ears. As the freshness tugged at him, his consciousness floated up from the depths where it had been flung, beyond sleep, beyond death; and he felt the pain wrench his dead heart as his scarred palms grabbed the edge of casket. He heard his backbone creak as he struggled to sit up, and moist coolness stung his cheeks, perhaps morning dew, perhaps his own tears. Through the wetness, as the casket lid slid open, he saw in the grey light the clenched faces of the two Sanhedrin Elders whose names he had forgotten, but whose eyes had remained chiselled in his memory.

"How many nights have I slept?" he rasped, sitting up in his bronze-lined sarcophagus. "Two nights? Three?"

He knew it was still night because the sky beyond the crypt's marble doorway spread blue-black and dull like a dead snakeskin pockmarked with stars; and behind it, like vertical stains of ink, rose the spiralling towers of the city of Bashan. Then all at once, as the smell of dried blood and putrid wood shavings came in his nostrils—the smell of the gallows—his memories flooded back, like skittering crows plunging down to perch on a leafless oak.

"So I have been pardoned?" he whispered. More wetness stung his cheek.

The two Elders said nothing, just helped him climb out of the casket, their silken sleeves cool and slithering, their palms trembling as they touched his corded forearms.

"Take your armour and all your weapons," whispered the younger Elder. "Make haste."

Dutifully Og dug his claws under his crumpled cape, at

71

the casket's side, where his long sword, still in its bejewelled scabbard, lay besides his steel longbow and a dozen feathered arrows—the poison-tipped ones that he himself had dipped in the green blood of desert vipers. With numb fingers he felt for his steel dirk, the throat-slasher, the hook-spiked flail, the brain batterer, and all his other equipment made illegal by Sanhedrin law. Even as his mind sought for answers, his hands were already acting of their own accord, distributing the weapons about his huge body, each item in its designated cache. "Why can't I leave my weapons here?" he asked. "The bailiffs won't let them into court." He flung the scabbard's wide belt across his chest, letting the sword hang along his back, buckled the iron clasp, then slung his long bow with one mighty twang, while the two robed Elders watched him in silence. The younger of the two, Og saw, was watching with something akin to anger. The older one watched with blank equanimity. Both smelled of camphor and balsam and perfumed water. The Temple's smell.

"Will the Sanhedrin's session last long?" Og asked. "Or has my appeal been accepted already, and this is a mere formality?" He stood up, stretched his hirsute arms, bent his knees several times and yawned. His body was stiff as if he had slept years, not just a few nights. His claws, he saw, had grown overly long, and the dark stains under the tips were now dust.... A violent shudder went through him as the red memory slammed into the back of his head, and the understanding. "No court session?" he croaked. "No pardon?"

"No court," the younger Elder said, spitting the words through tight white lips. "We came because—we—the Sanhedrin—we need your help—again...." He breathed in spurts, his eyes narrow with distaste and hate.

Og sank down on the edge of his casket. His corded neck throbbed where the woven metal rope had tightened around it last time. And the time before that, and all the times before. Fiery red-tinged memories roared back, like an avalanche of lava. How many times did this scene happen already? How many times had they called him, and lied to him? How many times had he promised himself not to believe anymore? Has he not lost count?

"No!" he rasped. "Last time you also said you needed me! You swore it would be different! Yet once it ended, you again put me to trial for what I have done for you...."

"We had said it would be different if you followed instructions! But you disobeyed," the younger Elder hissed. "You did what we expressly had asked you not to do in war—never to do—we had told you...."

Og tugged his sword out of its scabbard, the blade tearing through the years of rust with a screech like a crow's. Pulling a whetstone out of its cache he began to sharpen the long blade. "There was no other way. There never has been! They hide behind their women and elders as they fight; they give poisoned weapons to their children...."

"No! There must have been another way."

"There was none."

"We gave you your instructions and rules of war and you ignored them—"

"There was no other way to save Bashan."

Why was he even talking back to the Sanhedrin Elders? It had always been thus. Og tested the long blade on his index claw. The sharp edge barely left a line. He went on sharpening, his eyes narrow and hot.

The older councillor spoke now, "Bashan needs you again." His voice was dispassionate, matter-of-fact, reasonable, as if speaking to a child, or a domestic animal.

Og kept on sharpening his sword. In the distance he heard a faint boom of cannon. He felt his blood freeze, then quicken.

"No," he said.

The younger Elder stuttered, "But...but the Midianite army has returned, and—and there's no-one else."

Og said, "Has the Sanhedrin at least heard my request for pardon, for last time's deeds?"

There was silence. The answer was clear.

"Why not?"

The senior Elder said in a coppery voice, "We told you. We could not condone such war acts. We simply could not."

"But I have done them all to save the City! They were all necessary! As always!"

The Elder shook his head obstinately. "We simply cannot condone such acts."

Og said, "But when you sent for me last time, you knew I must do something similar to the time before, to repel the Midianites. They do worse!"

"We are not them. Such barbarity, had we but known...."

"But you must have known!"

Again, there was silence, cold and fluttery.

Og put the whetstone away and slid his long sword into its metal sheathe. Now it slipped in noiselessly. He said, "I will not go fight for the City this time unless I know I will be forgiven if I do again what I must, to defend it."

The two Elders looked down, then at each other, and muttered softly. The younger one spoke. "We—we are authorized to accept your condition."

"You are?"

"Yes. If you defend Bashan, nothing you do will be held against you this time."

"Nothing? Even if I have to fight their children—if I have to do what I have done before?"

The two Elders looked away. "Hopefully it will not come to that."

"And if it does? With such evil enemies, it always does."

The younger councillor's whisper was nearly inaudible. "As we said, this time you will be forgiven."

More rumbling of cannon came on the night air, and a few piercing screams.

Og stood up. "How strong is the Midianites' army now?"

"Stronger than last time. Five new brigades of children have been formed, and not only their arrows, but their teeth too are now dipped in poison...."

"And ours? Bashan's army?"

"Feeble. Feebler than before."

"Why have you not re-trained? You have had how long? Three days? A week?"

"Seven years."

Og sat down in shock. "I have—slept—seven years?"

No answer.

"In seven years you could have trained Bashan's entire army to fight the Midianites and do the necessary deeds like me—"

"No, no!" The younger Elder's voice held traces of panic. "We cannot allow ourselves to teach such things! If we did, we would be no better than the barbarians!"

Og remembered he had had this conversation many times before. It was useless to argue. He rose to his feet. "Where are the Midianites camped?"

"We'll take you."

When he at last came back, covered in grime and blood and brains, they were waiting for him at Bashan's gate.

"You have won?"

"Yes." He was cut in a hundred places. His talons dripped blood. His teeth too. Gashes over his eyes were encrusted with grey-yellow muck. "I have killed them all."

"All?"

"Yes."

"How?"

He told them. "It was the only way."

"But we have told you expressly not to act this way! We have told you to adhere to the conventions of war! No atrocities, we said! Haven't we?"

Behind, he saw, a crowd of Bashan city folk was gathering, dressed in victory silks of white and blue.

"No you haven't," he said to the Elders. "You told me to do the necessary, to defend the city, and whatever I do will be forgiven."

"We certainly will not!" the younger Elder said frostily, looking him straight in the eye. "We are civilized—unlike the barbarian Midianites you have just butchered. Some things we simply won't do!"

Og knew what was coming. "At any rate, Bashan is safe. Can I go back home now, to the hills of Moab?"

"The Sanhedrin will have to decide."

Next morning was the trial.

"Seven years ago," said the Sanhedrin's speaker, the presiding judge, "you committed war atrocities. Now you have done so again, against express warnings. I judge you to be hanged, then buried inside a bronze-lined casket. May every decent Bashanite abominate your name. You are an example of what we will never let ourselves become. Take him away."

As before, they hanged him before sundown, at the city's gate, with a rope of corded steel. When he stopped twitching they wrapped his body in his velvet cape, and one by one all the Elders came by and spit on him, carefully. Then two ageing bailiffs threw the body into the casket, slid the lid into place, and secured it with chains.

"His name should be a warning to all decent Bashanites," said the judge.

They had wrapped his body well, to preserve it. Just in case.

Authorization

"Sit down, Mickey, sit down.... You know why we are here."

"Yes sir."

"And don't call me sir.... Normally, the Authorization Committee meets only once, but this time they asked me to sit with you one more time...to go more deeply into what happened in this take-down in Paris, last month, before they can issue your Authorization...."

"So I was given to understand."

"Don't take this tone with me, ya-Mickey! I know you came in first in the course, and everything. Just because your father was the Mossad's Chief before me...it means nothing in this thing here, believe me. It's touch and go for you now, so I suggest you lower your nose a little and answer all our questions...where the hell are my glasses?"

"Here, sir."

"Yes, yes.... All right. You know Menachem here? Menachem Har-Even?"

"Well, he used to come have tea with Dad, but I never...."

"Yeah, all right...well, Menachem retired four years ago, so he knows only the old procedures but—yes, nu, someone spoke to the PM, and he said he also wanted Menachem in the follow-up, in case anyone later claimed you didn't get a fair...."

"Why? I didn't ask my dad to speak to the PM, and I really resent...."

"Shut up, Mickey! Just shut up! Okay? You just tell us whatever we ask...."

"But I already told you everything that happened...."

"So what? What we want is go into what *didn't* happen, and also why.... Yes, Menachem? You have a question maybe before we begin?"

"Just a clarification, Itzik, just a small thing. I mean, Mickey Ben-Attar was in Paris how long, when this happened?"

"Uh, Mickey?"

"Two weeks. I was there two weeks."

"So then you became Number Three, in the team?"

"Number Two."

"Two? Without an Authorization?"

"Yes. I was told that...."

"Itzik, pardon my ignorance, but did the procedures change since last...."

"No, Menachem, they didn't, but it was an emergency, like I told you twice already. We just got the word from the embassy resident *katsa* that Abu Salach had arrived in Paris for a meeting with the PLO executive, and would stay for one day only, two days max. So there was no time to set up a full take-down. We even had to borrow two guys from Zurich, from another Op which...."

"I understand, yes. But Number Two? Without an...."

"Menachem, do me a favour, all right?! Listen to what I am telling you, it was either this, or let the fucker disappear. Abu Salach himself! And like I told you, Mickey just came first in the course, he was tagged for Take-Downs from the second week...yes, Mickey, I believe you were told...."

"No I wasn't."

"So maybe they didn't want you to get an inflated.... Yes, Menachem? You have another question maybe?"

"I was just wondering if *katsa* Ben-Attar had ever before refused an order, or otherwise indicated in any way...."

"No, he didn't, and this is why we are meeting now. If we can begin, finally? Or you have some more questions? From the Talmud maybe?"

"No, no. All right, Itzik. Begin."

"All right? Fine, then.... Mickey."

"Yes sir?"

"Why don't you tell us again what happened in Paris last month."

"But I already told it four times, sir, the last time just yesterday, to the Authorization Committee.... Look, you want to kick me out, fine. Just tell me, I'll go. I mean, fuck this! This is worse than Jail Check, if you don't mind my saying...."

"Oh, shut-up, Mickey.... Menachem, will you tell him to shut the fuck up? I haven't got the patience for him anymore...."

"Relax, Itzik. Just relax. Okay? Mickey, listen. We only want to know why you made this decision, so it doesn't happen again maybe with someone else.... So just tell us again what happened, okay? why you didn't take him down when there was nothing to...."

"Like I said, I just didn't think it was a good idea anymore."

"Not a good idea anymore? *Anymore?*"

"No."

"Did you hear that? Menachem? That's all I wanted you to hear. Now we can...."

"Shut up, Itzik. Mickey, I am begging you. Why don't you save two old farts a heart attack and just tell us again everything, from the beginning, okay? For the sake of an old friend of your father, from the Camps? That for 42 years...."

"Okay, okay, okay! But you know anyway what—okay, all right! Last month I was told...."

"When exactly?"

"It was Friday, May twelfth...."

"When?"

"I already—okay, seven-fifteen in the evening. I was having supper with Dad...."

"Where?"

"At Hotel Lutèce, in Paris, in the courtyard...."

"You were travelling with him?"

"Yes...after I divorced Orna, because she couldn't have children, I moved back to Dad's apartment in Tel Aviv—since Mother died three years ago he's been living alone—so anyway, yes, we live together now, we also take trips, sometimes—he likes to see museums, theatre—what do I know why—but not alone—a hooker is not enough, he says —I don't know—so...."

"Wait a moment. Tell me, Itzik. When Moishe Ben-Attar was in Paris, he was also there for you, for something? I mean, is he still involved in anything, from here?"

"Involved? You crazy? You know the rules! Not from me. Maybe the PM asked him as a favour to pass a message to someone, what do I know. But me, I can't have anything to do with former...."

"All right, all right, I was just wondering.... Go on, Mickey. So you got a call from Itzik on May twelfth at seven-fifteen at the hotel Lutèce...."

"Yes. He called me and said...."

"In clear?"

"No, in NumberCode, that something came up, and that I should call one of the Zurich numbers to get instructions...."

"Ahh. So your dad did know about this."

"Well, sure—he was there when I got the call...."

"In the room?"

"Yes. We came up from dinner to take the phone call—he was planning to take me to a new whorehouse in Neuilly that someone in the embassy recommended, it's a place...."

"And your dad didn't ask you what the call was about?"

"No no.... He just said that if it's from the *ganef*, I shouldn't mind him, I can just leave and...."

"Ho ho. They still call Itzik the ganef? After 30 years?"

"I—I can't say, sir...."

"Don't call me sir. I am not your Bible Teacher."

"...Yes, all right...some still call him...."

"Look here, Menachem...."

"Shut up, Itzik, to be a *ganef* and a *drecker* for the Mother-land is an honour, so everyone else can afford to be pure... so what happened after the call?"

"I called the number in Zurich...."

"Which?

"The Gimmel number—it was a Tuesday...."

"All right, go on...."

"...and got the StringCode, and after I decrypted it...."

"Where? In the hotel?"

"No, in the toilet at the Chatelet Metro station...."

"Good...and then?"

"I took the Metro to the 19th quarter, to the Hotel Diamantine, room 235, like I was told...."

"That's where the team was?"

"Not a team, really, only Effie and Zerach...."

"That's Efraim Katchalnik and Zerach Toledano?"

"Yes."

"And then.... Yes, what now, Itzik?"

"They were following two PLO mules who were lugging some Semtex explo to Munich—the SDECE knew they were there, so...."

"The SDECE knew? Goddam it all to hell, Itzik! The SDECE *knew*!? You telling me now you tell the French *dreckers* what we—in my time, did we bare our ass before any...."

"Listen, you fart! It's *my* call who we tell things to! Okay? And we came to talk about Mickey, not about god-dam operational procedures.... You want to take this up later with Foreign and Defence, in the Knesset? Fine with me! With the PM? Fine also! But let's finish first this thing with Mickey here, because there are other...."

"You bet your pipi I'll take all this up later, after we... all right, enough for now.... So? Mickey?"

"Like I said.... I met Effie and Zerach, and they said they had just gotten the word from Tel Aviv that Abu Salach was arriving that night from London, and that it was up to us to take him down, if we could...."

"Itzik? That's so?"

"Yes, Menachem! That's so!"

"The PM gave the Go?"

"No need for it. Abu Salach was on the Permanent List."

"Not on the Annually Renewed?"

"No. After this attack on the kindergarten in Nahariyah, last month...."

"Okay, fine. And both Effie and Zerach have valid Authorizations?"

"Goddam sure valid, what do you think. Effie is six years with the Department, nine take-downs already, did the Refresher last year.... Zerach, he is in the *Sappirim* department now, but he was in Take-Downs up to February, so he still retains his Authorization, after...."

"Wait, Itzik, Sappirim is what, now? These NameCodes change so fast now, my brain can't...."

"Financial groundwork, bank accounts, money transfer...."

"Financial groundwork? So when did *he* do his last Refresher?"

"Look, Menachem, this has nothing to do with...."

"A year ago?"

"Look...."

"Two?...."

"Two and a half...but this is not why I made Mickey Number Two in the take-down...."

"So why did you make him Number Two? Because of his father?"

"Your mother's cunt, Menachem! Maybe in your day they played this kind of—Goddam it, I don't do things this way, and you know it! I told Mickey he should take a look at what was going on, see where he would fit in the team...."

"Putting him in charge?"

"Not in charge, just...."

82

"And what if he would have decided to make himself Number One? Eh? A fresh *katsa* just out of the course, without Authorization? In charge of a full take-down? In...."

"Listen to me...."

"...Menachem, sir...if I can explain...."

"Go ahead, Mickey. *You* tell us."

"There is nothing much to tell, Effie Katchalnik said he barely knew French, he was just passing in Paris on his way to Munich when he got the message to go to the safe-room in the Diamatine and wait. And Zerach, well, he was in Sappirim for a year, so...."

"Nicer and nicer, Itzik. Top *drecker* in the PFLP—you had no plan—Number One didn't know French—Number Two was an accountant who hadn't held a shooter in two years—you sent a fresh *katsa* without Authorization to take charge—and now you...."

"Menachem, shut up! What about in '55, when you sent the two kibbutznik kids to Cairo to blow up Colonel Machloof, without even...."

"But they did, and nobody caught them. In this business it's success that...."

"Well they didn't catch anyone this time either!"

"But they almost did. And if Mickey had taken him down—with the SDECE in the know—and...."

"Screw the SDECE! They had only two men in the hotel, junior Ops, both on the take. If Mickey had done what he was told, the first moment, we would have had Abu Salach pushing up poppies in some field in Sceaux, and everything would have been...."

"But it wasn't."

"Yeah, all because Mickey didn't...."

"Aw, Itzik, enough with this shit. Why don't we let Mickey tell it in his own way...."

"I was trying to, sir...can I have a glass of water?...yes, thank you,...that's enough. So, after I talked with Effie and

Zerach, finally we decided Effie would be Number One, and I Number Two, but if anyone had to talk, I would, because I had gone to *Alliance* High School, and knew French...."

"Sure, sure, of course...."

"...so then I called two local Jews that I knew from the time I was in Paris...."

"This was when?"

"In '77."

"In what role?"

"No role. I was just living there...."

"Itzik? I didn't know you sent people to live in a place before...."

"We didn't send him. He went there after the army, to paint...."

"To *paint*? Mickey?"

"Yes sir. For a year...then I came back...."

"Why didn't you stay?"

"I don't know.... "

"You still paint?"

"No...not often.... Fuck it, what does it have to do with all this?"

"Nothing, nothing...go on...."

"All right...so...where was I?"

"Effie was Number One and you were Number Two, but you would do the French-talking."

"...Yes, well, the order was very general, it said Abu Salach would be arriving at the 19th, from London, probably to the Hotel Mavrouq...."

"That's where?"

"On Rue Givernet, behind the alley with the Danish sex shop, with the dolls...."

"Oh yeah. So you waited there?.... Yes, Itzik?"

"Listen, Menachem...where they waited has nothing to...."

"Oh, shut up, Itzik.... Or you want me maybe to call the PM? To tell him you don't...."

"Forget it.... I was just...all right...."

"Good.... Mickey?"

"Well, we didn't wait in the street.... Right across there's a club on the roof, Moroccan place, cards and backgammon and zamzam...so Zerach put on a gallabieh and went up there, and from the roof...."

"Wait—how could he know if Abu Salach was...."

"Well, Abu Salach is more than two metres tall...so, if Zerach saw someone tall going into the Mavrouq, he would get angry and throw a backgammon chit out the window...."

"Get angry?"

"Yes, it's all right...these *Arabushim* get pissed all the time.... It's not risky...."

"How d'you know?"

"Well...like I said...I used to live in Paris, in '77...."

"And you used to go to the 19th? With the Arabs?"

"Uh...yeah...I mean, it's not like Tel Aviv...but they have falafel, and muja'adara...and it smells just like Yaffo sometimes...anyway, I know the area...."

"All right.... No, Itzik, you continue to shut up. It's Mickey's...."

"I just want to say that one of the reasons I called Mickey was that I knew he was familiar with...."

"Yes, yes, I noted it down. See? I wrote this right here. It's written. Now quiet. All right, Mickey, what happened when he.... By the way, was there any rehearsal before all this? I mean, a model of the street, the hotel, a timing chart, schedule of...."

"...Menachem, Mickey told you already there wasn't time to...."

"Itzik, I am begging of you. You really want me to call the PM? He doesn't like being called on Saturdays, have his snooze interrupted. But I'll call him now if you want, so he'll...."

"All right, Menachem, all right. I'll shut up. But

later...."

"Later is later. Mickey, go on."

"Uh, I mean, there was no model and no rehearsal—I tried to build something later on the bathroom floor...."

"With what?"

"Uh, with pieces of baguette, and...uh...some camembert...."

"Ho ho...bread and cheese model.... To scale, maybe?"

"I...I am sorry, there was no time...."

"Yes, yes...no time.... So what happened when Abu Salach arrived?"

"He arrived with his wife and girl at four-fifteen...."

"Wife and *girl*?"

"Yes sir."

"Girl? I didn't know he had any daughter."

"Neither did we, sir.... Menachem...."

"Itzik?"

"I can speak all of a sudden?"

"You can speak. You'd better speak. What's this about...."

"Well, I must admit we didn't know either.... It seems he married a Kazakh shiksa when he was in training in Tadjikistan, and later she tagged along with...."

"Seems? It *seems*?"

"Y...yes. We are checking now into...."

"Thank you for checking. Later we will..., yes, later. Mickey?"

"Like I said, he came at four-fifteen with his wife and daughter—we didn't know she was his wife then...only after...."

"Yes, yes...."

"They took three rooms in the hotel...I checked, he was staying in one room with her, the girl in another...."

"And the third room?"

"I am not sure...maybe for the meeting later...."

"You checked it all yourselves? Or you had a *Chipushit*

team do...."

"Ourselves—there was no time...."

"Ah yes. No time.... But you found out anyway...good... so what happened?"

"We...I mean, Effie and Zerach and I...first we cased the rooms in the afternoon...."

"Still yourselves? Where was the nearest *Chipushit* team?"

"...Let me answer that, Menachem...."

"You shut up, Itzik. Mickey?"

"I think in Ibiza.... Prince Fahed just came for two weeks to...."

"You think? You didn't have a printout before you left?"

"No sir, I mean Menachem.... Like I said, I was in Paris on time off, with my dad...so I wasn't fully...."

"Oh yes. You were there on time off, when Itzik reeled you in to oversee this take-down...."

"Listen, ya Menachem...."

"Shut up Itzik. Last time! You hear?"

"All right, all right. Only...."

"Mickey?"

"So we made a forced entry through the girl's room, and checked out the suite...."

"Why her room?"

"Because maybe he left something to be disturbed in his room...hair on locks, what do I know...something...."

"Sure he left something! What do you think they taught him in Tadjikistan for three whole.... Sorry, Mickey, not your fault. Go on...."

"But anyway, he probably knew someone had been there before, because when we came back later for the Op and barged into his room, at one-thirty...."

"That's AM?"

"Sure, at night, we had cut the wall in the girl's room, then glued it back, so it would be easy to re-enter. She was asleep, but when we...."

"Who's we?"

"Effie and me...."

"And Zerach was where?"

"In the hall...also with a Feinshmecker...."

"That's a Feinwerke? An air two-two?"

"Yes sir. We thought, from such a close range, a temple job is enough...no noise...no blood...."

"So why not a Beretta? With a silencer, in a plastic bag? Like normal people? Itzik, what's this thing with air-guns all of a—"

"Menachem, it was completely under the purview of the *katsa* on the spot to decide...."

"Ah, so now you blame Mickey for choosing the wrong weapon...."

"I am not blaming.... I am just pointing out he could have chosen anything...the embassy *katsa* would've...."

"O, all right, all right.... I suppose you're right on this one...let's go on...Mickey.."

"Yes, it was my choice...."

"Why not Effie's? You say he was Number One."

"Uh...yes...but I was to do the shooting, so...."

"Itzik? That's the procedure now? The shooter chooses? Not the team leader?"

"Yes, Menachem, it's called taking decision-making down the chain of...."

"Sounds like in-built ass-covering to me...."

"It's not ass-covering, it's...."

"All right. Your prerogative.... See? I'm open minded.... Yes, Mickey...."

"So that's it."

"What do you mean that's it? You were in the room, he was waiting...did he have a tool, or...."

"No sir, he was unarmed."

"His wife maybe? She maybe had...."

"No sir, she had nothing."

"So why didn't you shoot?"

"I...I...."

"Why?"

"...The...the girl, sir...."

"What about her?"

"She ran in and...she jumped in front of him...."

"So? So she jumped! Why didn't you blow Abu Salach?"

"I...I told you...."

"You mean the girl was between you and him?"

"Yes sir...."

"And the Feinshmecker bullet wouldn't go through? So what? First you take the girl down, then...."

"No sir, he hugged the girl...."

"What?...He hugged the girl?! The Arab fucker hugged his little *Arabusha*.... Listen, Mickey, maybe I was too hard on Itzik here, because the way this thing begins to look to me, you fucked up an easy...."

"No...I mean...shit in yoghurt! He hugged the girl... and then...then he put his hands on her head...."

"Ummnh?..., on her head...."

"...Yeah...."

"Mother's cunt.... So he put his hands on her fucking head! So what?"

"...and he said, 'In Allah I swear to thee, if thou shalt spare her, I shall lay mine arms down forever....'"

"Oh yeah? That's what he said? No kidding!...."

"Yes sir...I mean, No sir."

"He said he shall lay down his arms forever?.. If you spare his girl...."

"Yes...."

"He swore, too?"

"Yes...."

"On the Koran, maybe? He had a little green Koran to swear on...."

"No...no...he...he just said...."

"Ah...He just said.... And you did what?"

"I..., I said 'So Allah is thy witness?'"

"*You said what?*"

"I said, 'So Allah is....'"

"Yes...yes...I heard you...mother's cunt.... And what then?"

"And he said...Yes, so Allah is mine witness...by Muhammad's holy beard...."

"Muhammad's beard...I don't believe this...mother's cunt.... And so you decided to abort...."

"Yes...."

"By whose authority, if I may ask?...."

"I...what?"

"You are *katsa* on probation...no Authorization yet, Number Two on the team...you have no procedure-changing authority, yet you went ahead and decided to abort—by whose authority?"

"Authority? I...I just thought it no longer warranted.... I just couldn't...."

"Mother's cunt...you thought it no longer warranted..., and you just couldn't...well fuck me in the ass...I don't believe this...."

"Sir, it was just like I said...."

"Enough!...Enough!...Itzik, tell me, shall I strangle your katsa myself, or shall I let Moishe do it for us?"

"Sir..., Menachem...if I can just explain...."

"O, nothing to explain, Mickey..., nothing.... Itzik, I am sorry I was too hard on you...this country is going to hell ...bleeding hearts everywhere...well fuck me in the ass.... Yeah, what is it, Mickey?"

"Can I go, sir?"

"Go? Yeah...sure you can go.... I am sorry for your father, is the only thing I can say, but I can do nothing here...nothing...there's a limit...you're history, Mickey... history...."

Curse

After his second wife died also from cancer, my Uncle Getzl
left the Or HaNer Yeshiva in Bney Barak where my mother
was paying for him to learn Mishna and Talmud under a
grand nephew of the Chazon Ish, and rented for himself a
little room on the roof of No. 71 Shabazi Street, with only a
mattress, and immediately began to study cancer from the
Talmud and the Gmara and also the Poskim, to see if
maybe he could find there something, in case he got married again it shouldn't happen next time also.

The first month, my mother came every day to Shabazi
and cried and said, Getzl you should go back and finish to
study in the Yeshiva, because maybe it's all from God and
we shouldn't ask why. But Getzl said that cancer was only
from Ashmedai, and he, Getzl, was going to find out how,
to teach the Evil One a lesson, what it means to take two
wives from one man one after the other. When my mother
heard this, she said he (Getzl) should not speak like this, or
he could go too after the wives, he had a full life ahead of
him, he was only 43 maybe, that's young. But Getzl did
not listen to her, so finally my father said, Leave him alone,
maybe after a month he'll go back, and even if not, it's
cheaper in Shabazi than in the Yeshiva. So then they (my
father and my mother) had a big fight, and finally my
mother called a taxi to bring Rabbi Guthelf from Bney
Barak special to Shabazi (it cost nineteen Lirot). But nothing came out of it, because Getzl did not even open the
door and just said from behind it to leave him alone with
his grief, which is what he also said to the matchmaker,
that my mother brought the next week, just in case he got
interested. So finally finally that's what they did. Nobody
came, and every week I had to go to Shabazi to bring for
Getzl something to eat so he wouldn't die from hunger.

At first, when I came to bring to him to eat (some tchulent that my mother sent or maybe soup, or a piece of boiled chicken with farfel), I saw that he not only got thinner every day, but also more white from staying all the time in the inside of the room and only reading. So, like my mother asked me, I tried to talk to him, to see if he wanted something else maybe, or a fish, or maybe a challah, but Getzl said he did not want anything, or to talk to anybody, and he only made big sighs and said Ruchale, Ruchale my innocent treasure, Ashmedai should have taken me instead of you. (Ruchale is the name of Getzl's second wife that died from cancer, in the stomach.) But after two months, because I always stayed until he finished to eat, to take the plates and the pot back (so he wouldn't put the cigarette ash inside), Getzl began to talk from other things, which usually was cancer, and cancer, and more cancer, all from the Bible and the Talmud and also the Mishna, like I said, and how he was going to find everything out, but I didn't understand much, because this was three years ago, and I was only maybe ten, before my Bar Mitzvah even.

Now I have to stop and explain, because it's not really true what I said before, that Getzl only had a mattress in his room, because he also had an old bookshelf with books that he took from the Yeshiva in Bney Barak (or maybe they gave him, I don't know), and he also had three orange boxes that were once empty but that he filled with the copybooks where he wrote what he found about cancer in the Bible and the Talmud and the Mishna, like I said. So when I stayed to take the pots back, every time it was the same thing: first he offered me a Dubek cigarette, even that he knew my mother did not let me smoke (in the Yeshiva everyone does), then after I put the pot and the plates on the ice box where he ate from like a table, he took out from an orange box the copybook where he wrote what he read about the cancer, and told me the last things he just found, which if the doctors only listened to him, they would know about the cancer everything, and also maybe what to do, and then Ashmedai would have a *feig*.

For example, there was this Mitzvah with the Red Cow's ash from Deuteronomy, which the Grand Priest in the days of the Temple had to burn when there was a pestilence (if the people sinned, or even if not) and throw it (the ash) in the wind to stop the pestilence. And why? All because (that's what Getzl found in the Mishna) the ash could heal like an ointment or sulfa, from America, which his first wife at first also got. And why? Because everything if it could cause sickness, it could also heal it if it was done in the opposite way and not so much. Of this even Rashi knew, which was a big proof, because Rashi not only invented the Rashi script to write his explanations from the Bible and the Talmud in secret from the Goyim, but he also wrote explanations to the Rambam, who was the private doctor of the King of Egypt before Rashi was even born, or even the Malbim or the Radak, who also (both of them) wrote explanations to the Bible and the Talmud. So that's also a big point.

Anyway, this is what my Uncle Getzl found and this is what he told not only to me, but also to Doctor Pesach Rivkin, from Hadassah Hospital, because he (Dr. Rivkin) wrote an article in the newspaper Ma'ariv (page eleven) about cancer so that everyone would understand, in simple Hebrew. That's why Getzl wrote to him (Dr. Rivkin), because Ma'ariv is the only thing not in Yiddish that he reads sometimes, besides the Bible and the Talmud, like I said, and also the Mishna.

So Getzl wrote to him (Dr. Rivkin) that the cancer comes from ash, like from the Red Cow in the Pentateuch, which is clear not just from Rashi and the Radak, but also from the Mishna, and this is why to kill the cancer you also need to use ash, but in the opposite way, even if nobody knows how yet, and even if in the beginning it makes you a little sick, if you put in too much, because what's a little sickness if you want to cure the cancer? That's what my Uncle Getzl said he found, and that's what he told to Dr. Rivkin, in the letter. But the problem was, first of all, that Dr. Rivkin maybe didn't get the letter, and even if he did, that his secretary maybe didn't give it to him because she didn't understand about this, or maybe also from jealousy that he shouldn't listen to someone else, only to her. So this was the first problem. And the second problem was that Getzl didn't know how to write in Hebrew too exactly, so from shame he wrote to Dr. Rivkin in Yiddish, and maybe he (Dr. Rivkin) didn't know Yiddish, or maybe his secretary didn't know. So that's the second problem, and that's why he (Getzl) sent him (Dr. Rivkin) another letter, in Hebrew, which I had to help him to write, with everything from what he found. And from this letter the big problem started.

It started because after maybe a month, Dr. Rivkin wrote again in Ma'ariv (page fourteen) and said he just wrote to England an opinion that maybe cancer is from food and from smoking, and to cure it of course first you have to change the food and no smoking, but also maybe you have to drink special medicine like poison, that kills the cancer from the inside, which came from it first, nobody can know if it works or not until they tried.

So that's how it all started, because of this second article, and what happened was this: On Saturday morning at seven o'clock someone banged on the door of our apartment on Klonimus Street and shouted so loud, he almost woke up all the neighbours, and Mr. Farbel from downstairs even called the police (but luckily they didn't want to come just because of noise, it happened before). Finally my father opened the door, and before he could say Shabat Shalom, he (Getzl) rushed in and shouted at my mother (in the kitchen) that he wanted to take this Dr. Rivkin before a court, he (Dr. Rivkin) should be ashamed from what he had done, and also pay him (Getzl) damages for stealing his thinking, which he (Getzl) found all by himself from the Talmud and Rashi.

When he finished shouting and he sat down, my mother first gave Getzl to drink and a towel to wipe his face, then my father explained to him that a lawyer would cost him maybe fifteen Lirot an hour before he opened up his mouth even, so Getzl said all right, he'll take Dr. Rivkin to Din Torah, before the biggest Rabbis in Tel Aviv, he knew two of them from the Yeshiva in Bney Barak, so it was a big advantage from his side, and also he (Getzl) could speak there by himself without fifteen Lirot, because they (the Rebbes) knew Yiddish. But then it all of a sudden came out from my mother that she just remembered someone told her this Dr. Rivkin was a well known Atheist, so maybe he wouldn't even come when the Rabbis sent for him, it happened before. So did they need this, someone like him reducing their honour? And all because of Getzl?

So finally finally, after Getzl ate some chopped egg salad (with onion) and also some honeycake with Nescafé (half milk), he said that Rebbes or no Rebbes, never in the world will he forget from it, what Dr. Rivkin did to him, and Dr. Rivkin shouldn't think he (Getzl) will just pass on it just like that, without doing something to give him (Rivkin) back something, for all the grief he (Getzl Goldman) got from him, after he gave to him everything he found, for free.

My father then said that whatever Getzl had in mind sounded better than court or Din Torah, and he (my father) was happy Getzl was using his head finally, and then he shook his hand. Then after Getzl left (he took some honey cake in a newspaper, for Shabazi), my father said, See? You just have to talk to him like a normal human being.

But my father didn't know what he started, because next time I went to bring to Getzl something to eat (half a klops with sliced boiled egg inside, and also some calf-foot jelly, also with eggs inside), I saw that he had put all the Talmud and Mishna books in the corner under a piece of cloth, and he was sitting on the floor with some other books around him, from leather, it came out these were from the Kabbalah, I don't know where he got them, but probably from someone in the Yeshiva, they have to hide them anyway, in case the Rebbe will catch them, and then they'll have to say *Shma' Yisra'el* a hundred times, so why not give them to Getzl.

At first he didn't want to say why he got the leather books, but finally after he ate the klops (I also brought him some horse radish) it finally came out the reason he got them was because he was putting a big curse on Dr. Rivkin, after what he (Dr. Rivkin) did to him, even if it was only the *klafte* secretary, because he (Rivkin) was responsible.

Now I have to stop and say on the side that I was personally myself very interested in this, because all the curses I knew how to say were small little curses in Arabic, like *Kus Emaq*, which is (begging your pardon) Your mother's cunt, and *Yechrebetaq*, which is May your house fall down, and also one or two small curses to say in Yiddish that I don't know what they mean. But even when I said them all together seven times, with the name of Raffi Buchholtz that used to throw sand on my hair, nothing happened, he only threw more sand, and also when Ruthy Levin was watching. So when I heard this, I asked Getzl if I could maybe learn one or two small curses from him, from what he read in the Kabbalah, in case I would need them sometime for who knows what. But Getzl said no-one should curse just like that, without a big reason, because curses can sometimes bring up from the Tophet black angels and damaged spirits and other ruiners, so if you weren't careful and didn't know how to do it exactly exactly like the books from the Kabbalah said, like for example washing seven times in the *Mikveh* and saying *Shehecheyanu* prayer eighteen times, and other things that he didn't even want to talk about, because it was all secret, then if you didn't do all these things, maybe the curse would turn around and jump on your head, so then go get rid of it, and who needs it? Nobody. So that's why he didn't let me read in the books from leather, and only told me for a favour what he was going to wish upon Dr. Rivkin's head, that he deserved everything which he would get, because of the big grief he gave to others.

First, Getzl said, he asked for him (Dr. Rivkin), to become completely bald in the head like an egg, and also that the hair doesn't come back. And this is because without hair a man didn't have chances with women, even his secretary, which maybe Dr. Rivkin thinks he has, before his hair will fall off. This thing especially my Uncle Getzl knew from his own experience, from the time a younger widow (after his first wife died) didn't want to get married with him because he is also half bald in head (from too much Talmud).

So that's the first thing. Then second, he (Getzl) wished boils (*parech*, in Yiddish) upon Dr. Rivkin's whole body, like the *Sh'chin* in the Haggadah from Passover, that the Egyptians got after they said No to God, and this he (Getzl) asked not from cruelty, but only so he (Rivkin) should know how he (Getzl) felt all over the body when he (Getzl) saw in the Ma'ariv (page fourteen) what Dr. Rivkin wrote, without saying even one word how it all came from Getzl and what he (Getzl) found in the Mishna all by himself. So that's second.

But then the third and the biggest thing, Getzl said, he especially asked Ashmedai himself (which if he did this, he, Getzl, promised not to find about the cancer) to make Dr. Rivkin so he can't make children to his wife in case he had a wife, which Getzl didn't know if he had, or from the *klafte* secretary in case this was the one he wanted to get married with. And this third was the biggest biggest thing because (Getzl said) if a man couldn't make children to his wife she completely lost all the respect for him from the wedding and didn't wash or cook or even speak politely with him. So this would be the biggest result if everything happened like he (Getzl) asked.

When I heard all this I was very interested, like I said, and I wanted to stay to see how Getzl asked these questions from Ashmedai, even if Raffi Buchholtz said he didn't want to get married with Ruthy Levin, just in case he changed his mind. But then I had to go home with the pot and the plates so I couldn't stay, and I forgot to tell everything to my mother, because on the way back I had to go around, not to meet Raffi (for the last week he was trying to catch me, because of what I told about to him to Ruthy, even if it was all true, that he didn't want to get married with her.) So this is why I forgot to tell my mother about Getzl and the curses he was going to wish on the head of Dr. Rivkin, and that's why it was really my fault what happened later, because my mother had adjured me to tell her everything that her Meshiggene brother said when I went to bring to him to eat.

Finally when I told her (the next day) what Getzl said, about the curses, she stamped with her foot on the floor and said to my father (this was at night right after he came back from the shoe store), Come with me we're going to talk to this Shmeggegge and take him back to the Yeshiva I don't care if I have to tie him up with my own hands. My father said he wasn't going anywhere especially Friday night before he ate, because without eating he couldn't do anything, especially later. But my mother said there was going to be no later if he didn't come right now, and then I said I wanted to come too. Oh sure, my father said, let's take the neighbours also, so they can all see what family I got married with, and then there was a big fight with shouting. But finally my mother cried, so my father put on his black sandals and said All right, all right, just for you Malkah, and we took bus No. 12 to Shabazi and climbed all the stairs to the roof to see Getzl, and to take him back to the Yeshiva.

This was maybe eight o'clock in the night and the light in the hall didn't work, so it was Egyptian darkness, like it says in the Haggadah, and Getzl's bell also didn't work. So my father knocked and knocked, but there was no answer from anybody, so he said maybe he (Getzl) is asleep, this Smeggegge, from all the klops and tzimes. But my mother said He's not asleep, we would hear him snoring from downstairs (this is true), there is no noise from the inside of the room. So finally my mother took out the key that once she made a copy from Getzl's own key that Katchalski the landlord gave to her, and opened the door.

Immediately we got in I could smell such a smell like a stink worse than a dead cat or (begging your pardon) an outhouse in a Moshav, but we could see nothing, only Getzl sitting on the floor like an Arabush, with the legs crossed but the eyes open. My father went to him and said (begging your pardon), Getzl, Getzl, you farted all the klops? but he (Getzl) didn't move, so my father looked and looked, but the stink came from I don't know where. My mother right-away ran to open the window and the other door that goes to the roof where all the other people that live in Shabazi No. 71 hang the laundry, and immediately a big black cat tried to get in, but my father said Kisht! Kisht! and my mother said, I adjure you! and finally the cat left. Then she put Getzl on the mattress and with the broom she cleaned up all the pieces of paper on the floor, half of them burnt (on his head Getzl had burns too), and my father said, Go downstairs to Katchalski and say Isser (that's the name of my father) asks please for a half cup of maybe cognac or even cherry brandy, something strong. So I went down but I came back only with a quarter bottle of Carmel benediction wine (Katchalski said he didn't have something else), and my father said, It's even better. Then with the knife for the bread he opened Getzl's teeth and my mother poured the wine into his mouth. And then this is what happened, believe me because I am not lying:

First Getzl sat up like with a spring, then he shouted like a rooster two times, and finally when my father said, Getzl, I adjure you (my father never said this before, only my mother, because he said it's superstition for old wives), Getzl began to say Shehecheyanu, that a Jew should say only after he wants to say Thanks to God. But then (I heard it with my own ears) he also began to say HaGomel, which is what a Jew should pray (but he doesn't have to) if he got saved from mortal danger not from his own effort. My father tried to stop him and said, It's not for this, but my mother said Let him.

And then came the thing which I don't know how to tell, because my mother and father adjured me not to tell to anybody, so I'll only say that he (Getzl) became all wet in the pants. And he also began to cry from the eyes and the nose, and said he made a big sin, he should ask forgiveness in Yom Kippur. So finally we took him to downstairs, to Shabazi Street, then (Katchalski called a taxi already) to Hadassah Hospital on Balfour Street (luckily it's always open).

And now comes the best part, because who do you think was in the hospital in the night shift? I knew you'd say this, and you are right: Dr. Pesach Rivkin, that it came out he was also from Warsaw like my father, only he went to Auschwitz and my father only to Maidanek, and that's why they never met, but my father met his mother's cousin, in a Bar Mitzvah in Haifa. So he (Dr. Rivkin) said What have we here? The genius almost-Rebbe that sends me annotations to the Mishna in Yiddish how to cure the cancer and also diabetes? So Getzl said I never said diabetes, I only said cancer, and diabetes only maybe. Then he again cried from the eyes and the nose even more, and rightaway you could see he was sorry and regretted what he (Getzl) asked from Ashmedai about Dr. Rivkin, because he (Dr. Rivkin) was with only one eye and the left hand didn't move so good, it was probably from the Camps, so why add to his troubles, just because he had a secretary *klafte*? Also he (Rivkin) was already bald in the head worse than Getzl and he also spoke to him in Yiddish, so immediately you could see he was a good doctor that you can talk with him. (That's what my mother said later.) And to make it worse, it came out that Getzl's father (that's my grandfather Menachem-Leizer that went with Hitler) also was a good friend from the Cheder of Dr. Rivkin's brother. So when it came out all this, Getzl stood on the bed and shouted Upon my own head all I've wished upon the heads of the innocents! But then he had to lie down because everybody (also the two nurses) and my father and mother included, made him do it, and then a nurse gave him a little injection (I don't want to say where), and after this we left.

The next day, in the morning (it was a Saturday) we all came to visit but Getzl was in a different room, with a tube made from plastic going into his pyjama pants, he should not make his pants wet again, and bandages on his head because of the burns he got from the burnt paper, and also on his face, he could only eat maybe a little mashed potatoes, so what my mother brought, all the gefilte fish and the tzimes and the compote, my father said Good, now we can eat it, but my mother said No, she'll give it to Dr. Rivkin, he'll eat some and give the rest to poor sick people that don't have family. So then my father said Malkah (that's my mother's name), my treasure, where did I find you, and Dr. Rivkin (he just came in) said Nu, this you can do at home. So to make a long story short, that's why I didn't get to learn any curses from my Uncle Getzl, who after three days in the hospital ran away in the night back to Or HaNer Yeshiva, and after this he didn't want to say anything about curses when I asked him (except that nobody should say them). But because I went to clean his room and to take the leather books back to the Yeshiva, I read in one of them all about how to put a curse on someone that tries to take from you something, and maybe after Passover I'll try it.

Mish-Mash

In 1958 my uncle Nathan Berkovitch married two women and went to live with them both in Haifa until, a year after the weddings, a delegate from Haifa's Rabbinate caught up with him because of an anonymous snitch, and told him he must divorce one of the two or go to jail. Nathan, who was then working as a bookkeeper at the Haifa oil refineries, said he would divorce neither wife, because he loved them both, and what's more, they loved him too; and not only that, but both were pregnant (which was true), and how could you deprive unborn children of a father? Besides, the Yemenite Jews, who just two years before had been brought over to Israel from Yemen in a special operation, half of them had two wives, and not a few (mainly their rabbis) had three, and nobody in the Rabbinate said Boo. So how come? And why did they pester him, Nathan Berkovitch? Just because he was an Ashkenazi Jew? So maybe if he grew curly sidelocks and dyed his skin brown, they'd leave him alone? Huh? Huh?

Now, remember, this was just ten years after the founding of the state of Israel, when no-one made trouble for the authorities—who, as everyone knew, were busy building up the motherland. So Nathan's obstinacy was seen as both a sign of dangerous rebellion and scandalous apostasy. Rebellion, because he refused to do what the Rabbinate—an integral branch of the government—told him; and apostasy, because he claimed that he followed the Bible itself (—where all the patriarchs had more than one wife, and a few had concubines), and not the Bible's explicators and annotators in the Talmud and Mishna—whose opinions counted for him, Nathan, like the skin of an onion. And, he said, it wasn't as if he had a concubine. He had married both his wives legally and openly, before a real rabbi, who, even if he didn't know he was marrying the bridegroom for the second time without a Gett for his first marriage, still was a kosher rabbi, so the marriage held. Besides, the prohibition of multiple wives was not in the Bible, nor in the Talmud, or even in the Mishna. It was merely a thousand-year-old innovation by rabbi Gershom, the Diaspora's Luminescence, the very same one who had forbidden Jews to read letters not addressed to them—a dictum the Rabbinate's hirelings had broken sure as rain, when spying on him, Nathan. So how come the Rabbinate went by one Gerhomite dictum while ignoring the other? Huh? Huh?

All this, and more, Nathan said in the special Rabbinical Court session that he was forced to attend (without his wives). My father, who accompanied him, said that all this threw the Adjudicators for a wide loop. Because, let's face it, according to Jewish religious law, you can't force a man to divorce his wife, even if he's married to a second one. A Gett has to be voluntary on the man's side. If he refuses, you can only throw him in jail until he recants—but if he doesn't want to, you can't do anything, and his wife remains an unmarriageable woman forever. But could you do this here with a clean conscience? I mean, jail? If Nathan went to jail, he would surely lose his job (which, in 1958, was not so easy to come by), and then he couldn't feed his children. So who would feed them? The rabbis, maybe? They hardly had money enough to feed themselves. (This was before the coalition agreement that gave government stipends to all yeshiva students and exempted them from military service.)

And to make matters worse, both Nathan's wives—one a Jewish Yemenite named Miriam, the other a Jewish Iraqi girl (her name was Batya)—began writing letters (with the help of my father) to the then-Prime Minister, David Ben-Gurion (copies of which they sent to the daily newspapers), decrying the cruelty with which their husband was persecuted, while many Yemenite Jews, including rabbis (names enclosed) with three wives and four, went free. Finally, one day—this was in April, 1958, just before Passover—both wives (by then heavily pregnant) boarded the bus in Haifa and came to demonstrate before Ben-Gurion's house in Tel Aviv, until, pregnant or not, BG's wife Paula came out and chased them away with a broomstick.

The rabbis in the Haifa Rabbinate didn't know what to do. First, because there was the matter of bad publicity, which no-one wants even in the best of times. But to make matters worse, this was when demands began to be made for civil marriage—in Israel one can marry only religiously—before a rabbi, a qadi, or a priest—so the last thing anyone wanted, was a proof that the rabbis permitted polygamy, because in comparison, civil marriage would seem reasonable.

But how to keep this quiet?

For a whole six months, diplomatic delegations were sent to Nathan, beseeching him to do as he was told, and quietly. Divorce any one of the wives he chose—it would then be ignored if he continued to live with both, so long as he was legally married to only one of them. Why, didn't Ben-Gurion himself have his British mistress/secretary staying at his home, when she came to Israel to visit? Because his wife Paula preferred him sleeping with a woman she knew rather than with someone off the street?

Anyway, back to Nathan. First my father's cousins from Bney Barak, one of whom was head of a small yeshiva, went to see Nathan; then the other two, instructors in the Talmud sections of Divorces and Damages, went to see him, and all begged him, practically on bended knee, to give up, and not to make trouble. They even produced a special letter of entreaty written by R' Amatzia Sturman of Montreal, nicknamed the Second Luminescence and the greatest

Adjudicator of the generation, alternately beseeching Nathan and adjuring him to make do with one wife, like the rest of the Jews. But nothing helped, and in the meantime Nathan's sons (Ury and Pinchas) were both born, so how could he even hear of a divorce?

But then the problem got even more complicated.

The complication happened when Nathan applied for the Childrens' Grant that the government had just instituted, and in the routine check-up on his Living Conditions, a social worker was sent from the Haifa regional welfare office to see the two children. And this worker—her name was Hadassah Tzigler, a good Ashkenazi girl from Haifa's poshest neighbourhood—fell in love with Nathan (no-one knows why), and began seeing him clandestinely; and from here to there, Nathan fell in love with her also, and after two months he up and proposed to her—which, after much trepidation (because, having been to his apartment in her professional capacity, she knew about the other two wives), she accepted.

By that time Nathan's case was famous, even though the newspapers didn't write about it (there was strong censorship those days), so no rabbi would marry him and Hadassah. Also, and just to be sure, the chief rabbi of the Haifa region (R' Zalman Shaposhnikov, the brother of the famous theatre director) issued an edict that any rabbi who dared marry Nathan Berkovitch again would be cut off from the referral list of weddings, circumcisions and burials. Which meant he would go to the poorhouse. So nu, after a month during which Nathan went even as far as the southern port city of Eilat, to get a rabbi for his third wedding, he gave up, and finally decided that, if he couldn't marry Hadassah legally, he would make her his pilegesh—his concubine. This way, if and when they had any children, the children at least would not be bastards—which they would be if Nathan, heaven forbid, had slept with a married woman, or had married the divorcée of a Cohen. Luckily, to take Hadassah as a pilegesh, all Nathan needed was her consent, which he had, and also the means to support her—which he had also, since his first wife had meantime begun to work too (in Dubek Cigarettes, on HaNavi Street).

So finally finally, in July 1958, against the hysterical objections of Hadassah's parents (both secular teachers in Haifa's Re'ali High School, and both good Laborites), Hadassah went to live with Nathan Berkovitch and his two wives and two children, in his apartment in Kiriat Bialik, and the very next year she bore him twin girls (Malka and Rachel), and that's when the story began to unravel.

What happened was, Nathan's first wife, Miriam (the Yemenite), had slipped in the bath and broke the tap. (Luckily nothing happened to her.) So she called a plumber, a man by the name of Jacob Shleif who worked with Nathan in the refineries and also did plumbing and sold Payis lottery tickets on the side, and after he had fixed the tap, he sold her a Payis lottery ticket and stayed for tea, and they began to talk. From here to there, she also saw him by chance in the Supersol grocery a few days later, and they talked some more—and nu, it developed. How exactly, no-one knows. But a month or so later, Miriam came to Nathan and told him she wanted Jacob to be her husband also, same as Nathan was.

At first Nathan refused. Not because of what you think —because he would have to share Miriam with another man; but because in the Bible, where there are lots of precedents of one man living with many women (the Patriarchs, Kings of Israel and Judea, and especially King Solomon), there are no precedents of one woman living with several men, unless one considers Jezebel, or Potiphar's wife, or other shady types. So at first Nathan objected. But then Miriam said that if that's the case, then all right, she'll divorce him and go live with Jacob, and

Nathan immediately began to have second thoughts about his refusal. First, because he really loved Miriam. But second, and equally important, if he divorced Miriam, the Rabbinate's people would rejoice, and probably think they had managed to cow him. Yet my mother says that what really happened was, Nathan's other two wives—or rather, his other wife, Batya, and his pilegesh, Hadassah, went to him and said that what was good for him, should also be good for Miriam. Why should he be able to enjoy the favours of three women, when Miriam had to make do with one? So at last, after a month of negotiations in which my father, being Nathan's only brother, served as intermediary (Jacob Shleif, to his credit, did not stick his nose in), Nathan agreed to Miriam's request, and merely put forward one condition: that they all move to a larger apartment, since the three-room flat they were then occupying in Kiryat Bialik, was bursting already—what with him, Nathan, and three women, and four children. It was so tight, that children had to take turns sleeping in one bed, and women took turns sleeping in Nathan's bed. Once I heard my father whisper to my mother that he would not be surprised to learn that every now and then more than one woman slept in Nathan's bed, with Nathan. But my mother said no-one knows this for sure, and not to sin with his mouth. So who knows.

But to cut to the main point: in January 1961, Nathan sold his apartment in Kiryat Bialik, and he and his two wives (Miriam and Batya) and his pilegesh (Hadassah) and their four children (Ury and Pinchas, and Malka and Rachel) moved into a five-room flat in upper Haifa (on HaBonim Street, #13) together with Jacob Shleif, the plumber. Jacob and Miriam lived in one room, and Nathan in another. The other wife, Batya, and the pilegesh, Hadassah, as far as I know slept together in one room, and the kids shared the other two: the three boys in one room (Miriam in the meantime gave birth to another son, named

Immanuel, from Jacob), the girls in the other. Whether Miriam still shared Nathan's bed from time to time, I don't know; also whether Hadassah or Batya ever visited Jacob Shleif. Nobody ever talked about this in the family. But as far as my father could see (he went to visit several times), they were all happy there, until April 1963, when Miriam won 150,000 Lirot in the Payis lottery.

In those days, 150,000 Lirot was real money, something like maybe a million today. So the winning immediately threw the happy Berkovitch-Shleif household into deep schisms. Because even though everyone seemed happy and content before, as in every other family there were always little problems that could be blown up with the proper amount of bad luck. And 150,000 Lirot was a truly big piece of bad luck, especially when it came out that Miriam's winning Payis ticket had been bought with five Lirot she had borrowed from Hadassah. Or rather Miriam insisted she had borrowed the money—the five Lirot bill was lying on the kitchen table (Miriam said), and when she saw it, she asked Hadassah in a clear voice whether she (Miriam) could borrow it; and Hadassah (this Miriam remembered most distinctly) said Yes. So (said Miriam), all she now owed Hadassah—whom she loved like a sister—was the five Lirot, and nothing else. And to corroborate her claim, she brought forth the testimony of Batya, who had just come into the kitchen to fry an egg, and so heard Miriam utter the words, "Can I borrow the five Lirot from you?"

Unfortunately, Batya said in her testimony that all she had heard was, "Can I borrow five Lirot?" without "the" and without "from you," and, moreover, she did not hear at all Hadassah's answer, if indeed there had been one.

So this started the ball rolling, with Hadassah insisting she had not loaned the five Lirot to Miriam, and hinting that Miriam had taken it without permission, so that even a beginning rabbi could see immediately that anything bought with this money-taken-without-permission was hers, and hers alone. Same as the original money was hers, Hadassah's, to share with whomever she wished—which happened to be her two girls (Malka and Rachel).

Nu, you can imagine how it developed. Before long there was shouting and screaming, accusations and counter-accusations and digging up of ancient quarrels, and also, shame to admit, tearing of hair, and even fisticuffs. By that time, the dispute began to involve not just the immediate Berkovitch-Shleif family (Nathan, Jacob, Miriam, Batya, Hadassah, and the five children), but also my father, who was brought in as an honest mediator, and then my mother, who was brought in to explain to my father some of the women's words which at first seemed to mean not what he thought they meant, but just the opposite. So maybe two days a week, my father would close his shoe-store in Tel Aviv, and take the train to Haifa and return in the evening, looking haggard. And did he need this problem? Like a hole in the head he needed it. But what could he do? Nothing. He had to help his brother because all the other brothers (in Poland) went with Hitler—and also to keep it quiet, because who wants such family mish-mash to go out? No-one. At least (and this was the only blessing), the mish-mash was still being kept inside the Berkovitch family, because Jacob Shleif, to his credit, still did not bring any-one of his own into it.

And it all might have stayed this way, if not for one small detail. It then came out that the five Lirot that Hadassah had said were hers, were not really hers at all, but rather belonged to Batya's son Ury. It was the gift-money he had received in the Passover Seder the month before from Nathan, and he, Ury, then loaned it to his Aunt Hadassah (that's what the children called each other's mothers) so that she could buy Nathan a present for his birthday. And although none of this was in dispute—neither Batya nor Hadassah denied that the boy had loaned Hadassah the five Lirot—did this mean that the winning Payis ticket was really Hadassah's? Just because a boy too-young-to-be-a-witness (by the Talmud) had loaned the money to her? And even if this was so, did Hadassah now owe some of the winning to Batya's boy? And if she admitted even this, didn't she imply by this admission that Miriam also had rights in the money which she, Miriam, claimed to have borrowed from Hadassah?

To add to this mish-mash, Nathan, to whom the winning ticket had been entrusted for safekeeping, refused to give it back to either Hadassah or Miriam. First, on the grounds that he did not know who was right, and showing favour to either disputant would cast him in the role of a Dishonest Judge, preferring one side to the other, where he himself had a clear connection to both. But second and worse, he would thereby also become an Immoral Husband, by showing preference to one wife over the other. (The Talmud sages, like the Biblical Patriarchs, of course had several wives each). So Nathan said he would give the winning ticket to neither one, until matters were settled.

This raised the dispute to ever higher levels, involving progressively more members of the Berkovitch-Shleif family. At first Nathan's Bney Barak cousins came to give advice; then Jacob Shleif, for the first time, began to express his opinion too. (He was in favour of dividing the money equally, or at least equitably, although he was a bit vague abut who should be included in the first case, or what would be meant by the second.) Finally, Hadassah's parents waded in also, each offering advice, and girlfriends of Hadassah from the Haifa welfare office, each weighing in with a different opinion altogether. As a result of all this, my father's absences from his shoe-store lengthened to three days a week, and when he now left to arbitrate the ballooning dispute, he often took with him a Tel Aviv senior family court rabbi as an advisor in Jewish religious law. Once or twice my mother went along also (in which case I had to skip school and stay in the store); but nothing helped. The dispute only mushroomed ever larger, until it finally blew up when Batya claimed that Hadassah's and Miriam's claims notwithstanding, she, as Ury's mother, had natural rights in her boy's money, and acting as a Parental Fiduciary she could sue on his behalf before a Rabbinical Court —indeed, she had a moral obligation to do so, to protect his interest. And that's exactly what she finally did.

Two months after the Payis lottery win, when the mishmash was already good and ripe, Batya Berkovitch climbed on bus No. 301 from Haifa to Tel Aviv, disembarked on Allenby Street, and went straight to the Rabbinate's main hall, where, to the consternation of the old clerk (the father of Haifa's chief Rabbi), she lodged a formal Torah Suit against her Tzara—which is the derogatory Biblical term for The Other Wife—claiming Theft and Usurpation and Undue Coercion (via forcing a minor to testify against his natural mother), and several other complaints besides. And if that was not bad enough, Batya really threw the shmaltz into the fire when, the next day, she hired Getzl Goldman, my mother's crazy brother, (who has been studying unsuccessfully to be a rabbi for the past twelve years), as her rabbinical advocate, to plead her case before the Tel Aviv Rabbinical Court (Northern Circuit)—the very same court that had been trying for the past five years on behalf of the Haifa Rabbinate, without success, to force Nathan to divorce her.

Now let me make a little pause here. Because this Getzl, let me tell you, his name in the Rabbinate was mud. First, because he had never been formally ordained as a rabbi; and even though there is no rule that every rabbinical advocate must be a rabbi, that's usually the case. But second and worse was, that after twelve years of wildly ranging and unfocused study, Getzl knew so many obscure and useless annotations to the Bible and the Talmud and the Mishna, that, if he so wanted, he could show off most other rabbinical advocates as ignoramuses by raising useless objections based on past precedents no-one had ever heard of. This wasted everyone's time, having to go look for the citations (since Getzl was not beyond inventing imaginary sources), then refute them with other sources, a low trick that no true rabbinical advocate would employ, because then it could be done to him too.

But third and trickiest, Getzel only made his advocacy in Yiddish.

Now why was this so insidious? Because, in those days, there was the beginning of the coalition agreement that would in future provide to all yeshiva students no matter what age, free lodging and room and board (and a little stipend) and also exempt them from the army, so long as they studied the Torah. This was a very tantalizing prospect for yeshiva heads (most of whom augmented their meagre income with rabbinical advocacy), since the coalition agreement would flow more money to yeshivas, and so add to their income a little—let alone the further augmentation that could result from the power to exempt yeshiva students from the draft. So naturally these heady prospects made rabbinical advocates very cautious about how they appeared before the civil authorities; and the first step they undertook was to hold all Rabbinical Court sessions in Hebrew, rather than in Yiddish. This sudden Hebrew speaking was a bit hard on some old rabbis who spoke Yiddish only, and in dialect, while Hebrew prayers they knew only by rote—same as they knew the Bible. But with a view for the future good of the community, they all made the effort and adapted.

All, that is, except a hardcore conservative few, chief among them Getzel Goldman, who (begging your pardon) like old Catholic priests sticking to Latin mass, insisted on speaking Yiddish in rabbinical court also. So when Batya hired Getzl as her rabbinical advocate, it was clear to everyone she was ratcheting up the stakes by a threat that, if she didn't win her case, she was going to make trouble for everyone, cost what may.

The other wife and the pilegesh, Miriam and Hadassah, at first appeared in propria persona, representing themselves; but then, on the prospects of their share in the Payis winnings, they each got herself a famous rabbininal advocate: Hadassah hired the New York Boyberishe Rebbe's son-in-law (—and was *he* ever expensive!); and Miriam hired a Yemenite rabbinical advocate (who later became Israel's Chief Sephardic Rabbi). And these two, plus Getzl Goldman, soon flooded the Tel Aviv Rabbinate with so many indignant letters and submissions and counter-submissions and responses and objections and counter-objections, that two new clerks had to be hired, and then also a third, and of course also a Yiddish-Hebrew translator.

Now, you should remember that right about that time (May, 1963), the Tel Aviv Rabbinate had just merged with the Yaffo Rabbinate, and so had become the most powerful rabbinical court in Israel—more powerful than the Jerusalem Rabbinate, even. Naturally there was a lot of resentment against this powerful new court by rabbis everywhere, but especially in Haifa, which was then a "red" workers' town controlled by a wily Laborite apparatchik. Because of their "red" milieu, the Haifa rabbis were always an object of pity and condescension—to which sentiments my Uncle Nathan's double-marriage only added. So at first, the mishmash with the Payis ticket of the Berkovitch-Shleif household just increased the mirth in the Tel Aviv-Jaffa Rabbinate at the expense of the Haifa rabbis; which of course only augmented the Haifa rabbis' resentment. For a while this discord threatened to add to the conflagration, as Tel Aviv Torah briefs went unanswered and Haifa rabbinical

requests were quietly disparaged. So much so, that the chief
Israeli rabbi tried to mediate the dispute, but without success. Even adjurements (through letters) by the great R'
Sturman of Montreal were to no avail. But when the case
blossomed into what it finally became, both mirth and
resentment subsided fast, and the need for mediation evap-
orated, as the entire rabbinical establishment united in
defence against the potential religious-legal disaster.

And why disaster? Because right about then, there happened the first of those chance occurrences that turned the
"Payis Case" (as it later became known) into the biggest
and most complicated religious-law dispute in the history
of the Israeli rabbinical courts. So big and complicated, that
learned rabbis began arriving—at their own expense—from
as far away as Buenos Aires and Caracas and Gstaad, to give
their opinions—for free—about the Torah solution to all
this mish-mash, so as to save Jewish Religious Law from
itself. Only at the end, when Rabbi Amatzia Sturman of
Montreal, the Second Luminescence himself, arrived and
stood in the breach, did the danger pass. But until that
moment, there existed the possibility that the Gershomite
dictum against polygamy would be overturned, and with it,
all of R' Gershomm's other rulings—and with them, the
rulings of all Adjudicators who came after—and so all
Torah rulings of the last 1000 years would be undone. And
then where would all Jews be?

But let me not jump too far ahead like a goat, and tell
everything in order. Because right then happened the first
bombshell.

What happened was, in the middle of the second mediat-
ing session, Nathan suddenly announced that none of the
children was his.

Can you imagine?

When the uproar subsided, Nathan said that since the

children-who-were-not-his were all born while their mothers were married to him, they were all bastards according to the Torah, and so could not inherit anything—either from their mothers or from him—because bastards had no right to receive property from any Jewish person. (Talmud Bavli, Purity Section, chapter Gimmel.) So even if the children had acquired any property by chance, their mother(s) had no fiduciary part and/or obligation(s) in this regard either. And since in any case the money in question was originally given by Nathan to Ury, it was still Nathan's. So anything done with it and any fruit it bore from any use it was put to whatsoever, was legally Nathan's and his alone.

And even if—just suppose!—even if someone had tried to cast doubt about the origin of these five Lirot, any money lying on a table in the house was in the category of Found Money, as defined in the Talmud, and thus belonged to the Man of the House—namely Nathan Berkovitch—upon production of a valid title-deed to the apartment—which he had—and a marriage certificate—which he had also (two of them). So the five Lirot were entirely his, Nathan said, on at least two counts: the first actual and the second theoretical (though not less strong) and so the lottery ticket and the winnings thereof were his too, Q.E.D. And what other proof would anyone else with a head on his shoulders require? Huh? Huh?

Yet the above bombshell, as you surely know (if you read the papers), was of course not the end of it. Because in the meantime, although the Rabbinical Court filings are supposed to be secret, word had somehow leaked out to the lottery management, and the Payis directors realized that this could become a very hot mish-mash indeed. So right away they got themselves a civil court injunction, locking up the disputed funds in an interest-bearing escrow account in Bank Leumi, until ownership of the lottery ticket was clarified, either in a civil court by a judge, or by a ruling of a qualified rabbi in a Rabbinical Court, or by a fatwa of a qadi in a Shari'a Court, or via a government Order-in-Council—none of whom would of course touch the matter with a long broomstick.

In short, it was a real hot mish-mash as if designed by the Heavens to make trouble for poor rabbis.

And perhaps this was indeed the case? Who can say no? Maybe God indeed does do such things from time to time, to tell the Jews what they otherwise don't want to hear? Because even though there could still have been an amicable solution to all this, the second bombshell then exploded as if on cue. In the next joint-appearance of Nathan's and his wives and pilegesh in the forced-mediation hearing, Nathan stated to the chief adjudicating rabbi, R' Shaposhnikov, that not only Nathan's children were bastards, but that his wives had other men on the side, too; and so they were whores.

When Nathan said this word, all mediation was of course out of the question. And not only that, but when Batya heard Nathan say this word, she hit him on the head with her shoe's heel, and when he tried to hit her in return, Hadassah grabbed his hand and tried to hit him too (on the face); and then Miriam also hit him (on the chin), and tried to scratch his eyes. And when Nathan tried to defend himself, he pushed them off and both wives fell down. So Getzl Goldman, Batya's rabbinical advocate, intervened and pushed Nathan back and also slapped him twice on the face, the first on his client's behalf and the second on his own. And when R' Shaposhnikov's father (the court's clerk) tried to get in between to make peace, he was slapped by everybody. So his son (the Court's chief rabbi) ran down from the bench to defend his father—because the duty of a son to his father (as appears in the Ten Commandments) precedes the duty of a judge to his litigants. But it is also possible that R' Shaposhnikov remembered how Nathan had made laughing stock of the entire Haifa Rabbinate for five years, which is why he kicked Nathan five times. (My father says seven, but who knows.)

Be that as it may, in the big mish-mash that ensued, the police, shameful to admit, had to be called, and all brawlers, litigants and advocates were dragged out of the courtroom and driven in black police cruisers to the Abu Kabbir jail in Jaffa. And it is only because my father knew one of the jail guards (whose father was also from Radom, the Polish town my father came from), that they were all let out in the morning without having to go see a secular judge (for shame), and without bail, just on their own word and promise. (Also, my father later said, because of the coalition agreement. But who knows.)

What is sure, though, is that from that moment on, the mish-mash spun out of control. That very same morning Nathan asked Miriam to leave the apartment and to take Jacob with her. But—listen to this: she said No! Especially after what Nathan had said about his wives having men on the side—did anyone ever hear of such a thing? She had every right to stay and clear her name (she said), and also get what was due her: her share in the Payis lottery ticket, and her share in the apartment, and also a big apology.

Jacob, to his credit, still did not mix in it, and just said he would stick by Miriam no matter what. Nathan thought at first to throw Jacob out too, but because Jacob was a plumber and worked with his hands, and Nathan was only a bookkeeper and not too strong, what could he do? Nothing. So Jacob stayed; and when Nathan tried to order Hadassah and Batya to leave, they also said they were staying, to look after their property and their children, and, like Miriam, to defend their honour and good name. And if Nathan didn't retract his slander, there would be another Torah Suit, they said, only this time for libel and evil tongue. And how would he like that? Huh? Huh?

That very day in court, both Miriam and Batya said they wanted the suit for slander to proceed in parallel with the Payis Ticket Case, and insisted on filing the papers that very noon. At the mention of yet one more Torah Suit, R' Shaposhnikov (who after a night in the Abu Kabbir jail, was completely sick of both Tel Aviv and the litigants and only wanted to go back to his family in Haifa), shouted that there would be no further lawsuits. And when the women (or rather their advocates) insisted, R' Shaposhnikov screamed at Nathan, and ordered him to retract his allegations immediately or at least say he hadn't meant what he had said! But Nathan, obstinate like a mule, refused to retract anything—not a single word. He insisted everything he had said was true—true like the sun at mid-day and the moon at night—so he would retract nothing. If his two wives wanted to sue him, let them. He would prove everything he had said.

R' Shaposhnikov threatened Nathan with jail (which rabbinical courts can do) if he didn't recant, but after a night in Abu Kabbir, was this such a big scare for him? No. So Nathan kept refusing to apologize and again offered to prove his words were true. And when the judge hollered at him that proof of that nature was very hard to present in a rabbinical court, Nathan asked for a delay of a day so he could get his own rabbinical advocate to help.

R' Shaposhnikov nearly broke down, but had to agree. After all, how can you prevent a Jew from getting proper Scriptural advice?

And so the court adjourned, and next day Nathan returned with a rabbinical advocate who was the grandson of a great Safed kabbalist, and this advocate, the very first time he opened his mouth, dropped the third and biggest bombshell of all.

Before the dense crowd of shocked lay people and rabbis

(many from as far away as Berlin and Geneva), Nathan's advocate said that Nathan was (tfu tfu tfu) sterile. His seeds were so mish-mashed, that they couldn't swim. So even though Nathan could still favour women (else why would they marry him?) he was completely unable to beget children.

When this came out (my father said), you could have heard a skullcap drop in the courtroom. And when Nathan's advocate, with a modest flourish, produced a certificate from Dr. Rivkin (from Rambam Hospital) proving this both in Hebrew and in Yiddish, and with his signature and two government stamps too, there was a collective gasp and a shudder in the court. Because, can you imagine? A man with two wives and a pilegesh—and sterile?

But after the shock subsided, came the obvious question: so whose were the four children?

R' Shaposhnikov (the court chairman) began to question Nathan, not gently, and little by little out came this: first off, Nathan said he had told both his wives at the beginning about his affliction, and he had told his pilegesh as well.

So (asked R' Shaposhnikov), why did they agree to marry you, and Hadassah to come live with you?

Maybe, Nathan said, because I was otherwise all right (on which adjective he refused to elaborate), and also because I had a good job. But because every family needs children, to fulfill God's command to multiply, we all decided we'd get good seed from someone else—a friend maybe, or a volunteer—and mix this seed with mine, and use this mish-mash with a syringe, like with (begging your Honour's pardon) cows in a kibbutz. And who knows? Maybe God will smile upon us?

And that's exactly what happened, Nathan continued (after the gasping died down). When the wives got the seed from the volunteer and mixed it with Nathan's, by a miracle it worked, and God did indeed smile upon the two wives and upon the pilegesh, and they all got pregnant immediately. So this was why the children were all bastards, Nathan said, and the lottery ticket belonged to him alone.

Nu, you can imagine?! When finally came out all this, in more detail than I wrote here, the courtroom in the Rabbinate became like the Carmel market, everyone shouted together, and two elderly rabbis from Bney Barak fainted and had to be taken to Beilnsohn hospital. (But after they got Valerian to smell in the ambulance they made the driver stop driving, and straightaway ran back to court to hear the rest.)

Then of course happened the inevitable: With this last revelation, no detail of the case could be kept out of the papers any longer. First, *HaOlam HaZe*, Israel's first yellow rag, published a cover story about the "Ashkenazi Yemenite" from Haifa and his many wives (they made it four wives, and not just one pilegesh but two), and his winning ticket (they made Nathan the winner, and in the soccer pool, not the Payis lottery, and of a quarter million Lirot; but the other parts they got correct.) And a day after *HaOlam HaZe* came out, *Ha'Aretz* (which is like the *New York Times*, only even more Liberal) also printed the story, but in a restrained manner; and finally finally also came *HaTzofeh*, the paper of the religious party, which wrote a long article about the entire mish-mash. (They were also the first ones who called it by this name.) And this article got *HaTzofeh*'s editor fired (because of all the enraged letters the publishers got from rabbis' wives), and so his assistant got his job. And then the fired editor got himself a civil lawyer and sued *HaTozfeh*'s publishers (which at the time was the Rabbinate itself) in civil court—can you believe this impertinence?—because who has ever heard of one religious

Jew suing another before the secular authorities? It's a scandal! Who is above whom here?! And all of this because of what? Because of a Payis ticket and two wives and a pilegesh and a second husband?

Yet two days later, as the trial against the Rabbinate (launched by the fired *HaTzofeh*'s editor) was gearing up, there happened worse: When the Rabbinical Court's clerk asked Nathan, for the record, who were the friends whose seed he had mixed with his to beget his bastard children, Nathan's two wives and Hadassah sprang up and began to scream and yell, adjuring Nathan to keep quiet. But some yeshiva boys in the crowd helped the court-guards to restrain the women, and so Nathan could speak. And when he finally spoke, he said that (as you may have suspected) the volunteer had been none other than Jacob.

This was no longer such a big shock. The shock was what came after, which was this: Jacob Shleif, who did plumbing for the refineries and also sold Payis lottery tickets (and pencils and New Year greeting cards too), also made money on the side donating his seed to the Seed-Bank in Rambam Hospital, where Dr. Rivkin (the brother of the famous cancer doctor) was treating infertile poor Jews to help them multiply. And Nathan, who had known about this because he worked with Jacob in the refineries and also had fought alongside him in the War of Independence, in '48, asked Jacob if he would mind if Nathan took this seed for his wives—because it was better to get seed from someone you knew was healthy, and also not an Arab, than from a stranger. The problem was, normally if you went through Rambam hospital to get seed, the donor remained anonymous, because Dr. Rivkin was in the middle like a veil. But if you asked for someone you knew, then maybe he would feel badly when you met him later in the street, or at work? But Jacob said he didn't care, and Nathan said, if you don't,

I don't either. So that's what happened. Nathan asked Dr. Rivkin to give Jacob's seeds to his wives, and that's how Nathan's first four children were born.

But after a while, Nathan began to think about it, and he said to Jacob, Why do we have to go through Rambam? I can pay you directly—more than what you would get if we went through the Hospital and Dr. Rivkin took his cut, but less than what I would pay Dr. Rivkin.

Nu, because Payis tickets and pencils didn't exactly sell too well that year, Jacob said all right, how much will you pay? Nathan mentioned a price, but Jacob said he wanted more, and they could not agree. So finally Nathan said, Come to the house tomorrow, we'll talk about it. But to prevent the evil tongues from wagging in case something became known, when Jacob arrived next day it was as-if-to-fix the tap that Miriam as-if-broke. This was the plan. But what wasn't in the plan, was that when Miriam saw Jacob (she never saw him before, only his seed), she fell in love with him, which nobody could foretell (only God can). So what can you do? Nothing.

Now when came out all this, four more rabbis fainted (all from Haifa), and R' Shaposhnikov, who was just about to announce a recess, nearly fainted too. But just as the fainted rabbis were being carried out on litters (R' Shaposhnikov refused to be moved), Miriam jumped to her feet, pushed her advocate aside, and, waving her arms in the air, shouted that all right, since Nathan told this part, she'll tell the rest. All of it!

From surprise, one of the carriers dropped his litter (the rabbi who fell later sued him), and the three other carriers stopped so the fainted rabbis could listen. And lucky for them, because Miriam's next words threw the case into the very high orbit that threatened to wreck more than ten centuries of Jewish Torah law.

According to Miriam, the truth was this: when Jacob

came in, he first drank tea (which she made for him), and was very polite to her. Then she left the kitchen, and Jacob and Nathan immediately began to haggle, because what Nathan offered was still too cheap, and what Jacob wanted was still too high. Only after an hour Jacob finally came down to 40 Lirot for his seed (he had begun at 80), and Nathan came up to 30 (he had begun with ten).

Here R' Shaposhnikov had to quiet the courtroom repeatedly, and issue several threats to the rabbis' wives who clicked their tongues ever more loudly each time a new detail came out. When silence was finally established, R' Shaposhnikov asked Miriam how she knew all these details. How? she said. How could she not? Nathan and Jacob argued loudly in the kitchen while she was in the nearby bedroom darning children's socks (the children were in school). So she heard the entire thing to the end, when Nathan and Jacob were only five Lirot apart—Nathan said 35, and Jacob still said 40. But then Nathan broke the deadlock by saying, All right, 35, and you can contribute your seed to Miriam any way you want. Jacob said he was agreeable—but only so long as Miriam agreed too.

At this point the court had to be recessed for an hour and some screaming spectators cleared out, including two reporters. And when the court reconvened, Miriam went on and testified that when she overheard this, she decided immediately to agree—not because she wanted to sin with Jacob (whom she'd just met), but to take revenge on Nathan who had valued her honour at five Lirot only.

When came out all this tall-tale, R' Shaposhnikov was so overcome, that he had to be taken out on a litter, and one of the four other adjudicating rabbis, R' Simcha Sturman, had to take over. This R' Simcha was a grand nephew of R' Amatzia Sturman from Montreal, the Second Luminescence, the very man who saved all Jewish Religious Law a week later. But let me not jump ahead, because right after R' Shaposhnikov was taken to hospital, came out the last bombshell (by Miriam), which was this: when Nathan paid Jacob his money, he gave Jacob four bills of ten Lirot each, since he did not have anything smaller. But because Jacob did not have change either, how do you think he gave Nathan change?

If you said with a Payis lottery ticket worth five Lirot, you are exactly right.

When finally came out this last part—and as it became clear that the entire story about the borrowed five Lirot had been a tall-tale, to save the honour of the Berkovitch-Shleif family—the ballooning legal mish-mash showed the first signs of what it was finally to become: a Kushiyat Tophet (a Hell-Problem). This is the Talmudic term for a hypothetical question composed by the Devil himself, that cannot be solved by the Torah's Laws, no matter how much the smartest rabbis might try. And why is such a Kushiya so dangerous? Because one of the Torah's cornerstones is the saying (by rabbi Tarfon): "Turn it and turn it, and everything is in it,"—meaning that every problem can be solved by the Halacha—the accumulation of Jewish Torah Laws—so a Jew needs no other laws to live his life. The direct implication is that if even one Jewish problem could not be solved by the Halachah, the entire edifice of Jewish Law would tumble down, as the failure proved that Jews also needed other laws to live by, besides the Laws of God.

And if this were the case (tfu tfu tfu!), were would Jews be? In a dark legal mish-mash, that's where, with both God and the Other One contending for Jewish souls daily, each claiming His law was better than the Other's in this one case.

Can you imagine?

Small wonder then, that the subject of Hell-Problem is one that only very few rabbinical scholars are allowed to study —and even so, only after the age of 40. Just like the Matter of the Chariot—the flaming chair carrying the divinity that the prophet Ezekiel saw on the bank of the river Kvar in Babylon—and just as the study of the Kabbalah and numerical Combinations is restricted. All because—in theory—these subjects have the potential of ruining a Jew's faith by falsely proving to him the existence of rules besides Jewish law that are necessary to sustain life.

But since some readers of this tale may be too tender-minded to contemplate such lofty matters, or maybe too young, let's say no more of this and go back to the story, where, more and more, it now became apparent to everyone that what had begun simply with a Payis lottery ticket, a man with two wives, one pilegesh and a co-husband, has developed into that legendary rabbinical nightmare—a Hell-Problem that might not be soluble by the Jewish Halacha alone.

Matters began to deteriorate rapidly soon thereafter, when Jacob Shleif also got himself a rabbinical advocate (from Be'er Sheva), and this one now claimed that, Miriam's testimony notwithstanding, his client (Jacob) had not handed the ticket directly to Nathan. Rather, when Jacob had finished giving his contribution to Miriam (in a jar), he left the ticket on her bedside table (under the jar). And it was this ticket, not the one that Batya said she had bought with the five Lirot, that won the lottery. So theoretically, since the ticket was given to Miriam, it could be construed as Etnan-Zonah, payment-to-a-loose-woman for services rendered, and so belonged to Miriam, not to Nathan or anyone else.

Pandemonium would be too weak a word to describe what took place in the courtroom after this revelation—which was conveyed directly to the government that same after-noon. Because by that time, several government observers were already coming every day to see how the matter was developing, as the trial and all the noise surrounding it were slowing down the coalition negotiations with the religious parties. For how can any responsible official negotiate for yeshiva funds, when no-one even knew whether what was taught in yeshivas would still be valid tomorrow? Perhaps no post-Bible religious rulings could hold up before the hellish theoretical onslaught now taking place on Allenby Street? Maybe tomorrow's yeshiva boys could not even study the Talmud, or the Mishna? Perhaps they could study only the book of Genesis and nothing else? Or maybe only Genesis' first chapter? What then of all the crucial chapters in Exodus, Numbers or Deuteronomy, where God promised the land of Canaan to his chosen people? What then?

This, and more, came up in furtive whispers between spectators in recess, and in mutters over tea glasses in the court's kosher cafeteria, where pale rabbis stuttered hoarsely about the danger to the last 1000 years of Jewish Law—perhaps to the very patrimony!

Matters became so tense, it was said, that the Prime Minister himself (Ben-Gurion) was receiving daily briefings about the trial from the chief Israeli rabbi, whose beadle attended every court session and took notes.

Not that he needed to—there was so much written about the trial in both newspapers and magazines (though the radio of course said nothing), that the Prime Minister could have read it all by buying a newspaper. Matter of fact, the entire country was talking about little else besides the Lottery Ticket Given as Whore's Payment by the Man who Came to Favour the Wife of the Sterile Man with Two Wives and a Pilegesh. Even the secular newspapers dedicated whole sections over the weekend to readers' suggestions on solving the insoluble Kushiya of deciding who the winning lottery ticket belonged to. Because underlying all the frivolity, was the very real dread that, if this case could not be resolved by the Jewish Hallacha, then all Jewish

Torah Law of the last 1000 years would be in trouble—
perhaps even all Jewish Religious Law from the days of the
Babylon Exile. And where would the Jews be then? Huh?
Huh?

It was then that the matter was brought to the attention
of R' Amatzia Sturman of Montreal, the Second Luminescence himself (who already knew about Nathan Berkovitch
from the time he had been asked to adjure him to divorce
one of his wives, without success). And why was the question brought to R' Amatzia's attention? Because R' Shaposhnikov (the court's chief) was still in hospital, and so the
alternate head adjudicator was R' Simcha Sturman, the
S.L.'s grand nephew. And was this not another proof of
divine intervention?

Be that as it may, R' Simcha now prevailed upon the
other adjudicators to write to his famous great-uncle and
ask for his help. And so, a month after the Payis trial began,
the Tel Aviv-Jaffa rabbinical court sent the S.L. an urgent
telegram, both in Hebrew and in Yiddish, formally asking
for immediate guidance.

Although the Second Luminescence had just turned 91, and
his prostate had grown as large as an orange from the evils
of Canadian weather, he could recognize in the telegram's
entreaty the finger of God pointing to him a duty he must
perform. And can anyone refuse such a direct order? No. So
in the depth of the Montreal winter, R' Amatzia Sturman
packed his phylacteries bag, stuffed spare large underwear
into his satchel, and with the financial help of the congre-
gation's wealthier members (the Bronsky family) bought an
Air Canada ticket to New York; and from there, an El Al
ticket to Tel Aviv.

He arrived at Lodd airport on 2 February, 1964 in the
afternoon, and with the last of his Canadian dollars hired a
cab and told the driver to drive straight to the rabbinical
courtroom on Allenby Street in Tel Aviv.

When Rabbi Amatzia Sturman limped into the Allenby courtroom with his legs spread, nine rabbis, including five famous Safed kabbalists, rose from their chairs and prostrated themselves. His grand-nephew of course rushed to his famed great uncle's side, both to help him walk, and to be perfumed by his status, then offered him a seat by his own side, at the dais.

But R' Amatzia waved all admirers away, pulled a pillow from his travel bag, plopped it on a bench in the last row, and sat down carefully. Then, dismissing his grand-nephew back to the judges' table, he signalled to him with a wiggle of his spidery fingers to please continue and not to mind him. He was just a spectator in this court, he said; just as the Blessed Holy Name surely was.

At the mention of special providential attention to the proceedings, the spectators rustled with elation and panic, and a few rabbis' wives took out their Tzena u'Renas—the Yiddish translation of the Pentateuch. Even seasoned rabbis in the audience pulled out small Psalms books, to be on the safe side. For did not people say that at a word from the Second Luminescence's mouth, the angels themselves cocked an ear? Wasn't he the one-in-a-generation rabbi whose reasoned arguments in favour of studying the Matter of the Chariot (Ezekiel, chapter 1) were declared both valid and too dangerous to pursue? Was he not the one and only rabbi who, in the eventful year 1952, had dared decree that a bastard in the seventh generation could escape his stigma, and marry like any other Jew, by converting to Judaism as if he were a complete gentile?

This same juridicial daredevil now sat on his pillow at the back row, bearded chin in cupped hand, listening to my maternal uncle Getzel reason out loud why my paternal uncle Nathan Berkovitch should give up the Payis ticket— which was not a Whore's Payment as claimed by the other litigants, but rather a Thing Given unto Safekeeping by a wife who had entrusted her husband with a keepsake.

Getzel was well into his argument when R' Amatzia raised a thin forefinger and asked in Yiddish whether he could ask the plaintiff a question—just a little one.

Getzel's flow of words stopped in mid-vowel. The entire courtroom fell silent as everyone in the room turned back, and the spectators sitting in the front got up to stare backwards. My father said it was as if all adjudicators had suddenly emigrated to the back row, and everyone had to turn around for the trial to proceed. But the Second Luminescence did not seem to notice. He just stared mildly at my Uncle Getzel through wide blue eyes, and Getzl became all flustered and answered (in Yiddish) that of course the Second Luminescence could ask any question he wanted—he, Getzel would be happy to answer—

At which point the S.L. wagged his thin finger and said in broken Hebrew that he wanted to ask a question not of him, but of the plaintiff.

Getzel nodded shakily and sat down.

There was absolute silence in the courtroom, as everyone waited without moving a hair, as they say, until finally R' Amatzia asked Miriam in a very mild voice whether he could take a look at the lottery ticket in question.

Flustered, she said she did not have the lottery ticket—Nathan had it.

The S.L. turned to Nathan, who, to everyone's surprise, pulled a small envelope out of his shirt pocket and, walking slowly to the back row (perhaps to show he was not awed by any rabbinical eminence), gave the envelope into R' Amatzia's hand.

The crowd held its breath as the S.L. pulled out the checkered black and white square of paper, and held it up to the light in his emaciated fingers.

This? the S.L. asked in a mild voice. This is the object of contention?

My father said he felt like a cold fingernail on his spine, seeing this little paper that was threatening to sink ten centuries of Jewish Law. It was as if the presence of a Higher Being had entered the courtroom. But whether it was the presence of God, or of His Opponent—or maybe both—who could say?

All spectators and adjudicators gaped at the ticket, including the litigants.

Is this the object? The S.L. repeated.

Jacob Shleif said diffidently, What is the number, please?

R' Amatzia pulled a pair of narrow reading glasses from his frayed jacket and read out the number, first in Yiddish, then in Hebrew.

Jacob nodded, then Batya, and Miriam; finally Nathan gave a curt nod also. Yes, this was the ticket in question. The very same.

The air in the court became charged with electricity like Ezekiel's chariot, as the S.L. scrutinized the little ticket. But electricity turned into thrilled shudders as the old eminence raised his eyes and said that the answer to the Kushiya was very simple. In fact, he could not see why everyone had made such a mish-mash of it.

There was absolute silence in the courtroom as R' Amatzia went on and said that, not only was the answer simple, but it was in the original Torah, not the latter Talmud or Mishna. Why, could no-one present recall the relevant guidance given in very similar circumstances by that most famous of Biblical kings, who was wise in all things except in the matter of wives?

Feverish whispers flew through the audience. What answer to this Kushiya in the Torah was so obvious that the best Jewish minds of the generation had missed it?

A few rabbis took out notebooks; reporters activated their tape-recorders; and two rabbis' wives had pulled out lorgnettes—when a deep-throated gasp rose in the courtroom. Because R' Amatzia Sturman, the Second Luminescence, greatest Jewish adjudicator since Rabbi Gershom himself, pulled a pair of scissors out of his pocket, and put them to the winning lottery ticket.

All litigants began to shout at once. The four adjudicators cried out in alarm. The court's clerks, gasping, rose to their feet. Nathan jumped to his feet also.

Yes! Cut it! Nathan shouted. Cut! Neither I nor they will have it, but at least we'll live in peace, like before!

No! shouted Miryam. No! Don't cut! Give it to the children!

Batya and Hadassah, too, called to let the children have the winnings.

Yes, Jacob said simply. Yes.

It was, my father says, as if a great wind had blown through the courtroom. One moment panic, the second, elation. If before there had been sheer pandemonium, now there were joyous shouts, and heartfelt cries, and finally a few hand-claps that grew in volume until they turned into a feet-stomping applause. So much so, that two constables from police headquarters at Harakevett Street, more than half a kilometre away, soon burst in with their Parabelums drawn, a moment after the judgment had been given, to see what disaster had taken place.

But disaster, of course, had been averted, because judgment was handed down unanimously even before the applause died down. The Payis' winnings belonged to all children of the litigants, to be held for them in trust by the rabbinical court, who would oversee their equitable disbursal.

And what about the divorce? shouted the aggrieved R' Shaposhnikov, who had just come back from hospital to witness the very ending of the drama, whose final adjudication had not even been his. This apostate is breaking the Gershomite dictum! We cannot let him scoff at Jewish Law!

R' Amatzia, who had already begun to pack his pillow, said over his shoulder, I hereby permit Nathan Berkovitch to stay married to both wives. Unless either wife wants a divorce?

No, said Miriam. I love him even though he's a bastard.

And I too, said Batya. Both things.

Me also, said Hadassah. Even though I can't marry him.

But, shouted R' Shaposhnikov, overcome once more, it is a grave sin he is living in! And, he added in a choked voice, it is a sin to rule against the Gershomite dictum!

A sin? So let it be a sin, R' Amatzian said, his mouth twisting. For the Torah's sake, I hereby take the sin upon myself.

And so saying, he folded his pillow, stuffed it into his travel bag, and left the courtroom in a wide-legged limp.

Outside, as if by a miracle, a cab was already waiting.

Soon thereafter the matter died down. The Shleif-Berkovitch family returned to its Haifa apartment in HaBonim Street, #13, and within a year all women bore more children. Miriam bore twin boys, and invited the Second Luminescence to their circumcision ceremony. But R' Amatzia had died soon after the trial, and so R' Shaposhnikov was the godfather instead—people said he had not wanted to come, but was ordered to (some say by the Prime Minister himself), for the sake of reconciliation.

Who was the new children's father, you ask, Nathan or Jacob? What difference does it make, so long as the children received food and love, and were taught Torah and arithmetic and to be kind to others? What was important was that the children's family was not wrecked, and was even improved by the Payis' winnings. (Hadassah bought a piano.) And of course the Halacha was saved too, and so was the government coalition, because with the Torah Laws still valid, all yeshiva students, no matter what age, received free room and board at government expense, besides an exemption from military service, and also a healthy stipend. So healthy, in fact, that soon there were many more yeshiva students and more yeshivas had to be built, and taxes raised —including taxes on lottery winnings.

But this of course did not apply to Nathan's winning ticket—and luckily, too, because by that time, the Shleif-Berkovitch family's expenses had risen further, after Nathan had taken a second pilegesh (a rabbi's widow whom he had met during the court proceedings), and this one bore him two children. (The elder, who became a Shin Bett agent when he grew up, was the one who caught the truck loaded with explosives that nearly blew up the Knesset building with all members inside.)

Until they all moved to a house in Tel Aviv five years ago, the Shleif-Berkovitch family continued to live in the same Haifa apartment, where they also entertained my father when he came to visit and sometimes stayed the night.

But that's an entirely different mish-mash.